The Sixth Man

Anthony Dalton

Anthony Dalton Books

The Sixth Man

© Anthony Dalton 2017

All rights reserved.

ISBN – 13: 978-1545598474
ISBN – 10: 1545598479

Cover design by Steve Crowhurst
Cover images courtesy of shutterstock.com
Interior layout and design by Steve Crowhurst

Published by Anthony Dalton Books through CreateSpace

Font: Garamond 12

Printed in the United States of America

Thank you for buying an authorized copy of this book and for complying with copyright laws by not reproducing, scanning or distributing any part of it in any form without permission. In doing so you are supporting all writers.

For readers everywhere

ACKNOWLEDGMENTS

Many thanks to a host of American historians who documented the last days of the old west. A special nod of appreciation must go to author Robert Barr Smith for his detailed and thoughtful biography of the Dalton brothers – *DALTONS! The Raid on Coffeeville, Kansas.*

Thanks to my long-time friend, fellow author, photographer, artist and humorist Steve Crowhurst for designing the stunning cover for this book, and for the interior layout.

And, thanks to all my readers in many countries around the world who keep buying my books and asking for more. Without you my words would have little meaning.

AUTHOR'S NOTE

This book is a work of fiction loosely based on known facts about a notorious gang of thieves who created a considerable amount of havoc in the American mid-west during the early 1890s. Historical characters, who may or may not have lived at this transitional time, are used fictitiously. Any resemblance to any persons living or dead is purely coincidental.

I started thinking about writing this story while working on a magazine assignment in Arkansas. A day exploring Fort Smith and subsequent considerable research convinced me I should do so.

Although I bear the same surname as the infamous Dalton brothers of this story, I must make it clear that, as far as I know, I am not in any way related to them or to their descendants.

I'm not afraid. I never liked long lasting acts.
  -- Lillie Langtry

The Sixth Man

PROLOGUE

Howdy, folks. Deputy United States Marshall Heck Thomas here. I have a reputation for always getting my man, or woman – either one if they're outlaws – no matter how long it takes. I have spent much of the last twenty years of my life roaming back and forth across the west hunting outlaws and trying to find one in particular – a flamboyant criminal who called herself Flo Quick, among other aliases. She led me a hell of a dance. To find her, I roamed from Kansas to California and from Montana to Texas – and I reckon I visited every city, town and most of the ranches in between. Somehow that woman always stayed a few days ahead of me, until we finally came face to face late one brutal morning in South Dakota. That day, and over the next few days, I learned most of what there was to know about her. She sure led a wild life. Anyway, this is Flo Quick's story – told in her own words and in her own inimitable style.

CHAPTER 1

Twenty years ago this month the bullets flew in deadly haphazard arcs, like a storm of pissed-off hornets, on that otherwise beautiful autumn morning in Kansas. Yeah, it's two decades since four members of the dangerous and incompetent Dalton gang died in a blaze of violence. That was the day the handsome Bob Dalton screamed with pain and anger as the fatal bullet slammed into him and hurled him backwards into a pile of cobblestones. It's hard to believe, even for me, that a full twenty years have passed since four citizens of Coffeeville and four outlaws bled the last few seconds of their lives out in those dusty streets. History books, and there have been many on the subject, got most of it wrong. I can tell you the true story. I know what it was like. I know what happened, because I was there.

I'm the one the rumors called the sixth man. That's a joke in itself. If you could have seen me in those days, the way the Dalton boys saw me a few times – especially Bob – you'd know for sure I was no sixth man. My name? Take your pick. You can have any one of these because I have used them all: Eugenia Moore, Tom King, Daisy Bryant or, my favorite – Florence, or Flo, Quick. Yes, folks: that sixth man was me. I was tall and slim and, as the boys well knew, a full-breasted woman with a mop of almost black, curly hair hidden under a Stetson or a sombrero, depending on my mood. Me, a good-looking gal with dark brown eyes who somehow became known to some as the sixth man at the raid on the Coffeeville banks in October 1892. To understand my place in that infamous day we should go back a few years – back to before I met Bob Dalton.

I was a raggedy-assed wild kid, no doubt about that. Probably the product of too many drinks and a quick roll in a barn or a back alley: No love involved. No caring. Just a quick tumble with legs apart. As soon as I could walk, I was left to do almost anything I wanted – once I had done a few household chores. As far as I know, I never met my real father. I left home early, tired of being slapped around by an uncaring mother and pawed by a drunken scum of a so-called stepfather. If I had stayed, even though I was only a kid still trying to get used to the raging hormones of puberty, I would have killed one – maybe both – of them. I had to get out, for their sakes and for mine. Despite the troubles at home, I wasn't ready for absolute freedom but I didn't understand that at the time.

The day I left for good, on a whim really, without so much as a glance back at the untidy shack my parents called a house, I walked the few miles along a narrow dusty trail past barren fields where tumbleweeds played in the wind, and into town – first time I'd been there alone. There wasn't much there in those days, I don't even understand why people called it a town. Twin Mounds, in Douglas County, Kansas, was just a dirty main street with a row of tired clapboard buildings on each side. Behind them were a few houses, not much more.

I was hungry and thirsty by the time I got there. I had no money, of course, so I tried the sympathy route. I stuck my nose through the hotel's open door in mid-afternoon, hoping someone would take pity on me and buy me a soda pop, or offer me a cookie. Some guy in a suit chased me away. I tried the general store. The owner there always had lots of candy and other goodies, and it always smelled so good in there, but he just yelled at me and ordered me out – just because I was broke.

Later, with my stomach rumbling like a mid-summer prairie thunderstorm, I sat on the boardwalk near the saloon watching the men going in sober and, most of them, coming out drunk an hour or so later.

"Go home, child. This is no place for you," women told me as they passed. All they saw was a young girl with a dirty face and a scruffy dress. They couldn't see inside me. They didn't understand – I had no home to go to. Leastways, not the kind of home they were thinking of.

I kept looking at the horses hitched to the rail in front of me. Thinking. The horses stared back, twitching their ears and swishing their tails at the flies. Thinking, too, I reckoned. I've always been good with horses; even with mules and dogs. I knew I could charm any one of the handful waiting so patiently for their owners. There were few people about and no one was looking at me at the time. I stood up and walked over to the mounts, still thinking; wondering. I stroked a bay on the nose. She whickered at me. She looked strong, and fast. There was a bedroll tied neatly behind the saddle; a brace of bulging saddlebags draped over her withers and a shiny Winchester 73 slung along her side. Before I knew it, I had her reins in one hand, hitched up my skirts until my grubby long underwear showed and I climbed into the saddle. She let me do it. No complaints. She just let me do it.

There was no one watching so I rode her quietly towards the end of town. Past the jail at the end of the main street I let her have her head.

"Come on, gal," I yelled. "Come on. Let's git the heck outta here."

Well, we rode deep into the low hills that had given the town its name before sundown, I can tell you. Once I figured I was far enough away to be safe, I ate some stale bread I found in the saddle bags; had a drink of warm water from a canteen. As the night's chill descended on the land, I set a small fire and wrapped the bedroll around me.

I was fast asleep when a loud click woke me up. I opened my eyes to see night was fading; the sky was getting to be a pale gray color.

"Goddamned horse-thief! You'll hang for this, boy," a voice growled.

I came out of that bedroll so fast I almost pulled my dress off. Standing there with a six-gun pointed at my head was a young cowpoke.

"Now, what the hell is this?" he asked as he saw my long dark braids. "You a girl? Are you a girl?"

I nodded, so scared I thought I was gonna pee my drawers.

"Yessir," I nodded again. "I'm a girl. My name's Flo." It wasn't, but he wouldn't know that.

Well, this young cowpoke, he started to laugh.

"A girl. A fuckin' little girl stole my horse. Whaddya know about that?" He shook his head, still laughing.

"Sit down, girlie. I ain't gonna hurt you."

I sat on a rock, watching him, wondering if I could outrun him. One look at his long legs told me there was no chance. He holstered the gun and squatted on his haunches.

"You hungry?"

"A bit," I nodded, my stomach grumbling like an old bear. "Yeah, I'm hungry. I can make some chow, if you like. And good coffee."

He shook his head.

"I'll do it."

He soon had the fire going again, with beans and bacon cooking and coffee steaming. It sure smelled good to me.

"What's your name?" I asked as he handed me a tin plate of hot breakfast and a piece of hard sourdough. He ignored my question – just told me to eat. It didn't take me long, or him neither. As he finished wiping his plate with the last of his bread he looked up at me.

"How old are you, girlie?"

"Flo. My name's Flo. Not, Girlie."

"Okay. How old are you, Flo?"

"I'm fourteen, nearly fifteen. What's your name?"

"Fourteen goin' on fifteen. Hmm. Stand up, girlie. Let me look at you."

"I told you. My name's Flo, not Girlie."

"Yeah. Sure. Now stand up like I said, Flo."

I stood up. He motioned me to turn around. I did so, slowly, with my arms outstretched a little. He came closer. He didn't smell too good but then, I suppose, neither did I.

"What's your name?" I tried again.

"Don't matter none."

We didn't go anywhere that day. And he didn't turn me in to the law. Instead, he took away what was left of my childhood that morning before the sun was more than a pinch over the eastern plains. He was a young bull and he hurt, but I didn't let on. I just lay there under him with my legs apart and let him thrust away until he'd finished. Afterwards he rolled a cigarette, smoked it then sort of slept for a while, with one eye closed and the other on me. He kept his six-shooter in his hand, too.

I sat on his bedroll with my back against a stump of wood. We stayed that way for hours, until the heat of the day started to fade. Wakened properly by the cooler air, he had me twice more before sundown. That didn't hurt quite so much.

After a while, a few days I guess, I got used to him. Even learned to like what he did to me a little. I knew by then his name was Pete; that he was four years older than me and had just come off a long cattle-drive when I stole his horse. He must have liked me because we stayed together for a year or two, working on farms across Missouri and Kansas wherever hands were needed. I cut my hair short and dressed like a boy for the most part, so no one ever figured me for a girl. They just knew me as Tom King. By the time I was sixteen, of course, I couldn't hide the facts about being a girl. My breasts grew too big to be flattened properly anymore. It didn't seem to matter none to farmers. When they needed hands they didn't much care who they were, if they did an honest day's work. I could work all right, so that was no problem.

Then, just when we were planning to leave for Texas, soon after my seventeenth birthday, Pete got himself kicked in the head and killed by a wild stallion he was trying to break. I buried him myself in the hard, stony ground of Indian Territory, west of Fort Smith, and then I broke the stallion – but only after a long fight. I sold that demon for a couple of hundred and I was in business. I became a horse-trader – or a horse-thief, if you wish. And I was good at the job. I moved around a lot and sold my horses, usually at the open market in Baxter Springs – a small cattle town tucked away near the Kansas border with Missouri to the east and the Cherokee Nation to the south – far from where I stole them, so I never got caught.

I often called myself Eugenia Moore in those days, among other names. Eugenia was my favorite at the time though. It sounded classy to me. But, I changed my name so often, even I became confused. When asked, I had to think fast. Sometimes I would have Eugenia in mind and then Flo would pop out of my mouth. It's confusing but, hell, that was me when I was younger. I was Eugenia one moment, Flo the next. I never knew which one was me until I spoke.

A couple of years after Pete died, while I was in Fort Smith again after selling a few horses I had 'found' down near the Missouri-Arkansas line, I met the man who would change my life. I was enjoying the early autumn sunshine when I saw him. He rode in alone from the direction of Indian Territory as if he owned the town.

CHAPTER 2

I knew the man was an outlaw just by looking at him, but I couldn't turn my eyes away. He and the horse, a powerful roan, moved as one creature – almost lazy, yet in a natural rhythm. He sat straight and tall in the saddle and the roan held her head high and proud as she lifted her fetlocks with each dancing step. A couple of young boys played in the street, tossing a tin can high and trying to hit it with small stones. The rider unsheathed a Winchester rifle and fired from the hip in a single fluid motion. The bullet hit the can at the apex of its climb – dead center. Two more shots, both fired from the hip, hit the moving target before it reached the ground. By the time the perforated can stopped rolling the Winchester was back in its long saddle-holster.

I was leaning against a wall on the boardwalk outside a store. As usual in those days, I wore a check shirt, vest, work pants, leather chaps and cowboy boots – with a long, razor-sharp Bowie knife tucked inside one, plus a single six-gun slung low off my right hip and a rawhide bull-whip coiled up in my left hand. My hat, a black Stetson, was pulled low over my dark brown eyes to shield them from the afternoon glare. There was no way the rider could see that I was watching him so carefully.

He dismounted like a sleepy rattlesnake uncoiling and looped his reins over a hitching rail right in front of me. He looked me up and down as he stopped to light a smoke, and he smiled. He had the whitest teeth I had ever seen and the bluest eyes. He touched the brim of his hat with his right hand.

"Well, howdy, ma'am. My name's Bob Dalton," his deep, dark voice greeted me as if I had been waiting just for him; perhaps I had. I just didn't know it at the time. I straightened up a little and smiled back. I couldn't help it. Bob Dalton was a tall, handsome sonovabitch and he knew it.

He stood there looking at me and smiling all the time. Slowly he took the cigarillo from his lips and held it by his side. The smoke curled up his arm in thin blue waves.

"You dress like a man but you sure look like a woman to me," he drawled, still smiling.

"Can you use those things?" he pointed to my gun with the cigarillo, then to my whip, his eyes never leaving mine. The smile was playful, inviting.

"I can use everything I have," I answered. My voice sounded husky. Not quite like mine.

"I'll just bet you can," he grinned up at me, his eyes roaming down my body. I knew what he was thinking and grinned right back at him.

"What's your name, pretty lady?" The question came out like a sensual invitation. My brain told me to stay silent. My mouth didn't get the message so it lied, as usual.

"It's Flo. Flo Quick."

He nodded, his eyes sparkling; the smile easy and warm. I was hooked, and I had an itch only a real man could scratch. I spent the next two days and nights in bed with Bob Dalton and when we weren't taking care of my itch, he told me about the gang he and his brothers led, and he boasted about the 'family business,' as he called it. I'll admit it, I was impressed. I had lived on the fringes of the law since I was a kid. Bob Dalton was an exciting man and I liked outlaws: well, some of them anyway. I had no idea where this hot union was going and I didn't care. I was along for the ride wherever it took me. At that time and for a long time afterwards, I would have gone to Hell for Bob Dalton and, as later events proved, I damn near did.

CHAPTER 3

I don't think I'd ever heard of Coffeeville before I met the Daltons. I certainly had never been there. My preferred patch was the vast open plains between Arkansas and northern Texas, as far west as the beginning of the panhandle. That was a big enough area for me to work and live in. I didn't need to go to some town in Kansas where there were too many lawmakers. You know, sheriffs and deputies and posses of well-meaning citizens. I stayed away from busy places like that. Anyway, Coffeeville was still somewhere in my future.

Over the next few months after that first encounter in Fort Smith, I learned that Robert Reddick Dalton started life in 1868 in Cass County, Missouri, one of fifteen kids born to Adeline and Lewis. Two of the kids died young, the other thirteen grew up and some of them scattered off to western parts. Bob's eldest brother, Frank, was an honest man – a United States Marshall. I never met him. Someone said he was killed in a shoot-out with four horse-thieves out near the Arkansas River bottoms, in Indian Territory, in 1887. The only Dalton brothers I knew were Bob, Emmett and Grattan – usually shortened to Grat. Emmett, the youngest, was an outlaw but he was smart. Grat, the eldest of the three, was just plain stupid. He was an outlaw, too, but he had to be watched all the time because thinking was not one of his best skills.

All three of them were as tough as nails; they were all handy with their fists and never afraid to use them, no matter how big the opposition. Grat was also a hard drinker. I heard he'd been trying to destroy his liver with rot-gut whiskey and rum since before he was sixteen.

Some people said Bob could have been just like Frank, but his attitude interfered. Like his other two outlaw brothers, Grat and Emmett, Bob had a wicked temper that got him into trouble regularly. The three of them were bad news for regular folks, but Bob was often the worst. He was always ready for a fight. Hell, Bob Dalton could pick a fight in an empty bar. Strange then that he was always so good to me. He didn't try to slap me around the way a few other guys had. Of course, if he had tried it he'd have been dead too, just like them. I didn't carry a six-shooter for decoration. Years before, Pete had taught me all I needed to know about handling guns. By the time he died, even though I was still only a kid, I was a crack shot with both rifle and pistol. And the knife and bull-whip? Yeah. I taught myself how to use both and I am good with them, as anyone who touches me without an invitation finds out.

Not long after I met Bob, and later his gang, one of the members took a shine to me. Jim Davies was a weasel-faced little guy, but he was tough and fast as a striking rattler with his fists, and with his guns. Trouble is, he was sneaky but none too bright.

He tried to get me one afternoon at the Mashed-O-Ranch while I was forking hay down to feed our horses in the barn. Jim tackled me and threw me down on the hay, trying to kiss me, doing his best to get his slimy tongue into my mouth and rip my shirt open at the same time. The smell of his rotten teeth made me want to puke and his rough hands on my breasts hurt like hell. I slammed my knee into his balls and he got real mad.

His second big mistake was the first hard slap. It drew blood from the corner of my mouth and stunned me a bit. I came around to find him sitting astride my legs and undoing my belt and pants. I couldn't get at my knife and my whip was hanging off my saddle down below, far out of reach. I went for my six-shooter but it was gone.

"Get off me, you scum," I yelled.

"No way, baby. You are mine. Whooo-hoo." He bounced up and down on my legs in excitement, like he was riding some dumb bronco.

I spat in his eye. "Fuck off, you filthy little runt or I'll kill you."

Jim didn't like that. He punched me in the face and I saw stars again.

He had his belt undone and my pants half off when I came around for the second time. That's when I got real mad. I grabbed the front of his shirt and pulled him down on me fast, as if I wanted to kiss him. As his head came close I reared up and head-butted him on the nose. I heard it break as his blood and snot spattered all over me.

"You fuckin' bitch," he screamed. "You broke my fuckin' doze."

He swung wildly but the punch missed because I had wriggled out from under him. My pants were down around my ankles so I couldn't run, and my gun belt was somewhere in the hay where he'd thrown it. I stood and pulled up my pants with one hand and aimed a kick at his head. He saw it coming; grabbed my boot and pulled it off as he turned my leg aside. I fell sideways into the hay, my Bowie knife dropped out of the boot and landed in front of him. He got to it first.

"Well, well. Now lookee here. Miss high and mighty Flo's got a knife. Ain't that just dandy?" his voice sneered at me. I spat at him again and backed up as far as I could. He stood up, holding my knife at waist level and out to his right side a little.

"I'm comin' for ya, Flo. I'm comin' for ya. It's time to teach you a lesson. This time I'm gonna cut ya and then I'm gonna fuck ya."

He lunged forward and fell flat on his face as the snaky end of my bull-whip curled around his ankles and pulled him off his feet.

"Jump, Flo," Bob Dalton's voice called up from below. That was good enough for me. I kicked my tormentor in the head with my booted foot and jumped clear. Bob caught me in his arms. He was grinning all over his beautiful face as he kissed me then pushed me aside.

"Git yourself down here, Jim," he yelled, giving a mighty heave on the whip. With his ankles tied together, Jim rolled out of the hayloft and landed at our feet with a thump. Bob picked him up by his shirt and stood him upright, but still with his ankles tied.

"Go ahead, Flo. Hit him. He deserves it."

I didn't need a second invitation. I hauled off, clenched my fist and punched Jim in the mouth as hard as I could. It hurt me as much as it probably hurt him but it was worth it. He went over backwards into some horse shit.

"Pick him up again, Bob. I wanna hit him some more." I fell into a boxer's stance and started shadow punching. Bob laughed and stopped me.

"He's had enough, Flo. And, if you hit him again like that, you'll break your wrist."

I was still mad so I stepped past Bob and kicked Jim in the crotch. That made him yell again.

"Let it be, Flo. Let it be. I'll take care of it," Bob pulled me away. Then he reached down and dragged Jim to his feet. He held him at arm's length and said quietly, "You ever even think of touching my girl again and I will kill you." With that, Bob let loose a mighty right-hand punch and Jim went out like a light. He hit the ground hard and skidded right back into the horse shit.

I bent down to untangle my whip and said to Bob, "If you hadn't interfered I could have taken him, you know."

Bob just laughed and said, "Yeah. Sure you could, Flo." Then he walked away, laughing out loud. That got me mad again. I flicked out my whip and cracked the Stetson off his head. He looked back and glared at me. Before he could say anything, I got my mouth open.

"I said, Bob Dalton, I said, I could have taken him. Got that?"

I guess my pose must have looked suggestive because, before I could move, Bob crossed the floor, tackled me into a pile of hay and had one hand inside my shirt while the other undid my pants and ripped them off. With some help from my hands, he was inside me before a wolf could howl and I forgot all about being mad. I moved with him as he pumped at me and we moaned together. Over in the horse shit, Jim was coming around. He groaned in time with us and I got the giggles. Next thing I knew Bob and I were both laughing like fools, but we didn't stop. We came together with a scream from me and a gasp from him just as Jim let out a louder groan than before. The timing was so perfect, we became hysterical.

Later that afternoon, after I had retrieved my knife, six-shooter and gun belt, we were riding over to Silver City to meet the rest of the gang. Jim was still pissed off with me for breaking his nose, and with Bob for making it worse, so he was about a hundred yards behind us and complaining with every movement of his horse. I moved closer to Bob and rubbed his leg with my foot. I gave him my best smile and we both started grinning again.

"One of these days, Flo, I'm gonna take you on horseback," he warned.

I grinned at him and shook my head. "Oh, yeah," I said. "What do I need you for, mister? I've got a nice big leather pommel on this saddle. That's bigger than you and hard enough for me."

At the last word, I spurred my mare and raced ahead, laughing out loud as he cursed and tried to catch up. Way back in the distance, I could hear Jim yelling for us to wait for him.

CHAPTER 4

Although he occasionally used a small place near Guthrie, the Mashed-O-Ranch was Bob's main hideout in those days. He and the gang spent a lot of time in an old bunkhouse built for the cattle-hands years before. The cattle were long gone. So were the hands. The owners, Sadie and Thomas – both Irish, kept to themselves. I have no idea what they did for money, apart from what Bob paid them as rent. I had a feeling that they might have been on the wrong side of the law as well.

The Dalton gang was constantly changing in those days. At one time there were as many as eleven members, and they included Bob, Emmett and Grat, plus another brother, Bill – although I never met him, and Bitter Creek Newcomb, Black-faced Charley Bryant, Jim Davies, Dick Broadwell, Charlie Pierce, Bill Doolin and Bill Powers. Charley Bryant got himself killed by a Deputy Marshall out on the Indian lands in May 1891. So that cut the gang down to ten. Often, though, it was just Bob as the leader, plus Emmett, Grat, Bill Doolin, and the weasel – Jim Davies.

THE SIXTH MAN

As the winter of 1890 stretched into 1891, the Dalton brothers decided to go to California for a while, meet up with their brother Bill and see if they could find some action. I had some horses stashed away in the panhandle. I had to get rid of them so I stayed on at the Mashed-O. Bob promised to be back by late spring and then, he said, we'd have a summer of fun.

Soon after they left, I collected my horses – seven of them – and drove them clear across the plains to Tulsa through a series of snowstorms. It was hard going, for me and for the mounts, but we made it. With the weather so bad, none of the trading markets were open so I tried the livery stables. The owner, a huge bull of a man with a round head and no hair, introduced himself as Mr. Driscoll.

"Hi," I greeted him with my hand outstretched to shake his, "I'm Mrs. Eugenia Moore."

"What can I do for you, ma'am?" he asked, ignoring my hand.

"I need to sell seven of my horses."

Driscoll looked outside to where the horses stood in a line decorated with snowflakes. He looked back at me.

"Where's your husband, Mrs. Moore? Why ain't he selling the horses?"

"Oh, he's dead," I tried to look sad. "He took a fever at the beginning of the year and never recovered. I need to sell the horses, Mr. Driscoll. They're all I've got."

Well, we bargained back and forth for a while. Driscoll seemed to think he could cheat me because I was a poor widow. I knew damned well what my horses were worth and fought for a fair price. We finally settled on a figure that we could both accept. He took the horses and I took his money. Then he made another offer.

"You can rest out this bad weather in my barn, if you want. I can come by later and look in on you."

It sounded innocent but the look in his piggy eyes told a different story. I thanked him with a smile and rode away. He wasn't my type.

Bob and Emmett came back from California in the middle of March. I was back at the Mashed-O when they rode in. They and their horses looked just about all in. California had not lived up to their expectations and they had left in a hurry.

"We held up a Southern Pacific train in broad daylight near a place called Alila, in Tulare County," Bob told me. "There was supposed to be a lot of money on the train. There might have been, but there were also a lot of guards: too many guards for us to handle."

He looked really sad about it. Pacing back and forth in the bunkhouse, he continued the story.

"Me and Em, we got away. Grat and Bill were arrested. They're in the jail at Visalia for a long stretch."

He went on to explain that, while nobody got shot, there was a large posse of lawmen out looking for them, so Bob decided he and Em should high-tail it back to the safety of Osage County and the Indian Territory they knew so well.

The brothers were not a happy pair. Hoping to make big money in California, they had been disappointed and arrived home with empty pockets. I forgot to tell them about the money I had earned from the sale of my horses. That fact just sort of slipped my mind. The money was stashed away where Bob would not find it. I figured, what he didn't know wouldn't hurt him.

"We need a job and we need it fast," he insisted. "Flo, you'd better get back to work."

THE SIXTH MAN

Part of my job in the Dalton gang was to collect information about trains carrying money, such as gold, silver and big bank deposits. I was young and had a fine figure in those days. I always had the top three buttons of my shirt open because I liked to feel the breeze on my chest when I was riding. Of course, when I got into town I did most of them up again – unless I needed a display to distract someone.

I set up my first job for Bob and the boys that spring of 1891 at Wharton, a railroad station out in the Cherokee Nation on the Missouri, Kansas and Texas line, known locally as the Katy. Wharton was not much more than a few single-storey wooden buildings, a water tower for the steam engine and a large coal bunker. One of the buildings housed the telegraph office, with the water tower alongside it and the railroad tracks close by.

I tied my horse outside the telegraph office and strolled in alone to do some research. A railway man sat tapping away at the signaling machine. He glanced up at me, didn't seem to notice the open buttons on my shirt, and said, "Be with you in a minute, ma'am." Polite. I liked that.

I favored him with a big smile, even though he wasn't looking at me, and leaned back against the wall. While he worked, I opened two more buttons. When he finished sending his message and looked up at me his eyes almost popped out of his head. They only got as far as my cleavage and there they stayed. He stood up and knocked his chair over. He licked his lips, his eyes never leaving the focal point of my chest.

"Hello," I greeted him with a smile, my huskiest voice and an immediate lie. "My name's Eugenia Moore. I'm a magazine writer from back east. I'm researching a feature story on railroading out here in Indian Territory. I think you can probably help me."

He was good looking, in a rough sort of way, and he seemed to have some muscle on him. He was about twice my age but I thought, what the heck? I'll give him a real thrill. Bob was miles away and so were the rest of the gang. No one was gonna see us. No one else would know what I had to do. I needed information and this guy could give it to me. I decided to give him a present, up front, if you get my meaning. I reached behind me and turned the big iron key in the lock.

"What are you doing?" he asked, his eyes still hanging open somewhere lower than my shoulders. I didn't answer, at first. I smiled again and undid two more buttons, slow and easy. Then I said, in my lowest voice, "I'm supposed to be working, but I sure could use a good man right about now."

He got the message all right. His brain stopped working and his blood began to boil. I let him touch me and then I breathed, "Oh, you are so nice. What would you like me to do for you?"

While he was struggling to answer without letting go of his latest toys, I asked him about the trains. I had him in the palm of my hand at the time and he liked that so much he would have told me anything and everything, which he did.

By the time he'd finished babbling about timetables and freight, including bullion shipments, and I'd almost finished drawing all the information I needed out of him, I reckoned he deserved an extra treat. I dropped my pants and stretched out on the floor, taking him with me. He was good, I have to say that. He knew what he was doing and we moved together like rider and horse. About an hour later I left him smiling with delight as he tapped out a message on his telegraph key.

Later the same day, I passed on the information I got out of that escapade to Bob, missing out a few personal details, of course. Bob thought about what I'd told him for a while, worrying his teeth with a thin sliver of wood.

"Is this for real, Flo?"

"It sure is. There's a Santa Fe Railroad train coming along in two days and the telegraph agent said it will have a safe loaded with money on board, in the express car."

"What about armed guards?" Bob asked.

"Supposed to be two, both in the express car with the safe."

"Okay then. We'll hit it while the engine's taking on water."

Well, that one didn't work out so well. I didn't go on the raid because I would have been recognized and I had a couple of horses I wanted to sell anyway, so I was far away from the gang's action. I heard what happened later when we all met up at the usual hideout near the Mashed-O-Ranch.

Bob took Emmett, plus Black-faced Charley Bryant and Bitter Creek Newcomb with him. Grat, of course, was in jail way out in California. When the train stopped at Wharton Bob marched into the express car to discover there was no safe on board and, he soon found out, not much money anywhere else on the train.

By the time the gang had searched the two-carriages at gunpoint and taken everything of value from the passengers, they rode away with less than two hundred dollars each. And then Black-faced Charley got into a shooting match with the telegraph agent as they mounted up to ride away.

The agent fired a shotgun but missed everyone. As he rode past, Charley took a shot at the agent and hit him in the leg, knocking him over. The agent fired the second barrel as he was falling and peppered Charley's behind with shot. Black-faced Charley was killed soon after that in a shootout with a Deputy Marshall somewhere over Wichita way. I was secretly happy when I heard the news. I had enjoyed that telegraph agent fella and didn't like to think that he'd been shot.

We pulled a couple or more small jobs that hot, dusty summer while dodging the occasional tornado. We didn't make much money but we kept busy and never went hungry. We lived a nomadic existence, which I enjoyed. We rode throughout the Cherokee lands and parts of Kansas, to the Dakotas in the north, to the west almost as far as Dodge and south to Texas. We even took a couple of short excursions into Missouri and Arkansas to do a little banking. I didn't care where we went or what we did, I was just happy being with Bob.

In early September that year, Bob decided we should think about raiding trains again. That, of course, required my special skills. I rode the Katy line alone, looking at the possibilities of stopping trains between stations, or hitting them hard while they were standing still with steam clouding the tracks and the carriages. I liked the look of a couple of small stations and went to chat with the men in charge.

My first attempt at getting information for that month was almost my last. As I was getting to know the telegraph operator at Pryor Creek, some idiot burst in with a dirty old Stetson pulled low over his eyes, a kerchief over the lower half of his face and a six-shooter in each hand. Before he'd even kicked the door shut behind him, he was yelling something about a stick-up. I was at a distinct disadvantage at the time; so was the telegraph man.

I was on my back on his desk and he was between my legs with his britches around his ankles. I don't think that was what the masked man meant by a stick-up but the idea made me giggle a bit. Fortunately for me, and for the telegraph man, I guess, the newcomer was so surprised at the scene before him, he stopped in his tracks and said, "What the fuck…?"

Well, I thought it was kind of obvious, but I was too busy trying not to laugh out loud to say anything. Not surprising, the interruption had broken the lusty mood for both me and the telegraph man. He slid away from me as I reached my hand to my six-shooter, which was in its holster on the telegraph man's chair, right beside the desk. I grabbed my gun with my left hand, held it across my stomach below the waistline, a few inches above my skin, and pulled the trigger. I think I damn near shot the telegraph man's family jewels to hell. He jumped back just in time.

I rolled off the table to the floor as the intruder dropped his guns and spun in a circle, one hand hanging on to his injured arm.

Before he could recover I was on my feet and had picked up both his guns. He was swearing but his eyes were real busy. It was then that I realized my shirt was wide open. Everything I had was on display because I was naked from the waist down. I reached over to his face and pulled his kerchief down. He couldn't have been more than twenty.

"Take a good look, sonny," I crowed. "I'll bet you didn't expect to see a body like this when you burst in here, did ya?"

He shook his head; his eyes wide. "No, ma'am. I sure didn't."

The telegraph man pulled up his pants and did up his belt. He bound the would-be robber's wounded arm with a kerchief. He was gentle and seemed to know what he was doing.

"So, tell me, young fella," he said. "Why did you try and stick up a railroad telegraph station? There's nothing here worth stealing."

"I, uh. I, uh. I heard the railroad keeps money here for the train drivers, or something," he stammered.

"Well, now you know better. And soon you'll be going to jail."

The telegraph man took a coil of rope off the wall and tied the young man's hands and feet together.

"That'll keep him out of trouble until I can get a Marshall here to arrest him," he said to me. Then, without taking much of a breath, he said, "So, where were we?"

I was still half naked and, I must say, enjoying showing off my assets, but I had already got the information I wanted and I was not about to start again with a young audience.

"No, thanks," I said. "The moment has passed. It's time I was on my way. Thanks for the ride, pardner."

I pulled on my pants, buttoned my shirt, buckled my belt, holstered my six-shooter, put my hat on my head, gave the telegraph man a big smile and opened the door. As I was leaving I patted the intruder on his good shoulder and said, "You really are stupid. You remind me of someone else."

I tipped my hat to my most recent conquest, who was standing there with his mouth open, and left them together. Somehow, I had the feeling that that young robber would not be trying any more stunts like that for a while. One thing I knew for sure: he was gonna have a hell of a story to tell the U.S. Marshall when he arrived.

I had a look at two more railroad stops before riding on home to the Mashed-O. Bob was waiting and eager only to hear about trains and their value to the gang.

"Did you take a look at the possibilities at Laliaetta, Flo?" he asked.

"Yes. I went there after Pryor Creek. I walked along the station platform, what there is of it. There's a water tower at the south-west end. That's where the engine will stop, even if it doesn't need to take on water. I also had a chat with the telegraph man – he's also the station master. He's old and not likely to cause any trouble. And there'll be another train the day after. That's supposed to have money on board too, but for a different destination."

"Probably Tulsa," Bob said and then went quiet for a long time. He mulled over the idea for a few hours and then apparently decided it was too good an opportunity to miss.

"Okay," he agreed, at last, "We'll take the first Katy train as it pulls into Laliaetta. Emmett, you and me, we'll get the safe. The rest of you make sure no one tries to be brave. Flo, you'd better wait over at the Guthrie hideout. I don't want that station agent to recognize you."

I wasn't happy about missing the raid but Bob was adamant and he made sense, so I agreed to wait near Guthrie. I had some plans of my own to think about anyway. I left a note for Bob at the hideout and went to work. There were a couple of fine looking horses roaming loose not far from the town. I'd seen them twice recently. I figured, if the owner couldn't keep track of them, I might as well take charge. I reckoned they would fetch a fair price down on the panhandle. And they did. When I rejoined the gang a week later, Bob told me about the raid on the train.

"It went well," he said. "No shots were fired, so no one got hurt on either side."

The downside, he explained, was that there was not nearly as much money on board as expected. The boys rode back to the hideout a few hours after the raid with only just over $2,000 dollars to split between us. It wasn't much but it would sustain us for a few weeks.

I picked up a couple of newspapers on a quick visit to Fort Smith in early October 1891. One of the stories mentioned that the noted outlaw Grat Dalton had escaped from the jail in Visalia, California. I had no doubt he'd be riding hard for the east to meet up with his brothers. The idiot was coming home to rejoin the gang. The news depressed the hell out of me for some reason. There was only one cure for that. I went shopping.

You should have seen Bob's face when I walked in while he and Emmett were playing cards. I had on a new pair of Mexican chaps, a silver studded vest and a big white sombrero. I stood there looking at Bob with my hands on my hips. Slowly I twirled around.

"So, what d'ya think, Bob?"

He was trying to beat Em at five card stud and lost track of the game. His mouth fell open and he stared. I noticed Emmett was looking at me instead of his cards, too.

"Well. Do you like it or not?" I gave another twirl.

"Jeezus, Flo. You look fantastic," Bob said putting down his hand. "Emmett, we'll finish this game later. I'll be back in a while. Flo, you come with me."

We didn't go far, only to the next room. But we were gone for a long time. Bob and Emmett never did finish that card game.

CHAPTER 5

Well, we finally got rid of Jim Davies. It happened just after Grat came back from California in the late spring of 1892. You'd think Davies would have learned his lesson back in the barn when he had a go at me, but no, not him. I was about to mount up, my left foot in the stirrup and the other on the ground, when a hand slid up my leg and groped my crotch. Without looking I knew it wasn't Bob. I'd felt his touch often enough to know it well. I hoisted my butt high and kicked back with my right boot as I swung into the saddle. A satisfying crack told me I had connected. Next thing Davies was grabbing at my left leg. I looked down and there was blood all over his face from where I had just flattened his nose again.

"Come down off there, you bitch," he roared at me. "I'm gonna fuckin' well kill you."

Just about then, before I could get another boot into him, Bob kicked Davies's feet out from under him and he went rolling in the dust.

"Get up, Jim," Bob said. His voice was quiet and dangerous.

Davies stayed where he was and reached for his gun. Bob kicked it out of his hand.

"I said, get up, Jim." His voice was still quiet but now there was a real edge to it. Davies tried to crawl away so Bob booted him in the ass; then he stood over him, his hands hanging loose by his side.

"Get out of here, Jim. I don't need you no more. You're too fucking addle-headed for me."

That's when Davies really screwed it up. He propped himself on one elbow and looked up at Bob. Blood was running from both his nostrils. He spat a couple of times and wiped his nose with his sleeve.

"How come I gotta go," he whined. "Grat's stupid too. How come he gets to stay?"

I laughed so loud and hard, I peed myself.

Without looking at me, Bob said, "Shuddup, Flo. Or you'll be next." That made me laugh even more. Bob picked Davies up by his shirt front and said, "Go on now, Jim. Git, before I have to hurt you."

Davies still didn't get it. He pointed to Grat and said. "That's not fair. He's stupid, too. How come only I have to go?"

"Because he's my brother and you are not. That's why," Bob shouted.

Grat wandered over and asked, "Who's he calling stupid?"

Bob stared at him and shook his head. "You. You moron," he shouted. "He's talking about you."

Grat frowned and turned towards Davies, who was walking backwards as fast as he could. I put a stop to that. The end of my whip tied a knot around his ankles and down he went for a second time in as many minutes. Grat launched himself at Davies as Bob yelled at me, "Stay out of this, Flo."

With that he hauled Grat off Davies and sent him back to loading the horses. He untied my whip to free Jim's ankles and told him to leave while he could. Davies, the dumbest guy I've ever met, said, "Yeah, but what about Grat? Is he leaving, too?"

I laughed so hard, I peed some more. Bob lost it completely. He hauled back and knocked Davies off his feet with one punch. Out like a candle being snuffed. I was sitting there on my saddle, an uncomfortable damp patch spreading between my legs and I still couldn't stop grinning.

"What's so damned funny, Flo?" Bob's stern look set me off again. I snorted and coughed and gave him a belly laugh. He stood there by my horse's head, his hands on his hips, staring straight at my face. If he had looked down he would have seen what I'd done, but he didn't, at first. I snorted a couple more times and then spluttered, "I peed my pants."

At last Bob looked lower and a faint grin showed at the corners of his mouth. He shook his head in slow motion.

"I'm surrounded by fuckin' idiots," he said, "and she thinks it's funny, so she pees her pants. What the fuck am I gonna do with these morons?"

He stood there a moment longer, his eyes on mine. Then, he took a step closer and pointed at my middle.

"Flo," he said, "I think you'd better get down off that horse and get changed before you drown the poor beast."

How he managed that without laughing I have no idea. He turned and started to walk away. I slid off the saddle with my back to him; draped the reins over my horse's neck and followed Bob, my legs wider apart than normal. My crotch was very damp. He heard me coming, stopped and looked over his shoulder. As I passed him, I couldn't resist a parting comment. I winked and said, "Hi, handsome. I don't suppose you'd be interested in a little, you know, right now?"

That got to him. He laughed out loud; grabbed my arm, turned me to face him. He kissed me hard and then said, "Get some dry pants on, woman, and we'll talk about it." With that he patted my wet butt and pushed me towards the bunkhouse. I didn't look back but I could hear him howling with laughter as I waddled away.

CHAPTER 6

That night, while most of the gang played cards, and with me wearing clean and dry clothes, we talked about another Katy train, soon due in the area. I had checked all the schedules a couple of weeks before on a visit to Tulsa. Bob asked a lot of questions but all I could really tell him was that the train would be carrying money and the timetable.

"We could hit that at the Pryor Creek station," said Bob, thinking it through. "What date, Flo? And, what time is the train supposed to get to the station?"

"Two days from now. It gets into Adair at 9:42 p.m. and it's due at Pryor a few minutes after 10:30 p.m."

Bob lit a smoke and stood silent for a while. The boys carried on playing cards. I watched Bob and waited for his decision. It wasn't long in coming.

"I don't like the idea of going to Pryor. You've been there before and someone might recognize you on the station. We'll hit the train at Adair instead. And there's more places to hide there, if we have to."

I didn't bother to tell Bob that someone – namely a certain telegraph man – sure as hell would recognize me at Pryor Creek from a year before, especially if I took my shirt and pants off. I kept that snippet of information to myself, although I did smile at the memory.

Bob then began his routine of telling each one of us what our roles would be. I was supposed to be a backup and, as Bob said, "Flo, try not to get into trouble."

"Up yours, darling," I muttered under my breath but it came out a bit louder than I intended. Bob gave me a steely-eyed look which said far more than words. I shut my mouth.

On the evening of the raid, we left our horses in a shallow draw a few minutes west of Adair in care of occasional gang member Charley Pierce. Acting like we belonged there, we walked in along the railroad tracks. No one took any notice of us.

We'd all heard that the law was out in force looking for the Dalton gang all over Kansas, parts of Arkansas and in the wilds of Indian Territory. One name came up more than any other when the law was mentioned. The one man who, it was said, never quit looking. His name was Deputy Marshal Heck Thomas. I asked Bob about him as we walked beside the steel rails.

"Have you heard of him?"

"Yeah. I've heard of him. He's been on my trail for a while. Never gets close enough to take me down though. Don't worry about Deputy Marshall Henry Andrew Thomas: that's his full name. He and his two partners, Bill Tishman and Chris Manning, always come looking for me too late. Folks call them the Three Guardsmen. They'll never catch me."

Bob's confidence was comforting but the conversation bothered me. He might be able to stay out of the deputy marshall's hands by himself. The addition of idiots like

Grat, who could not keep his stupid mouth shut, gave the lawmen an edge that might tip the balance one day. I mentioned it to Bob.

"Don't worry about Grat. He's not as stupid as he looks," Bob assured me.

I didn't believe it. I'd seen Grat in action – mouth and fists – too many times to have any faith in his mental abilities. I knew, one day, sure as hell, Grat would let us down. I kept the thought to myself. Grat didn't need me to cause trouble between him and his brothers. He would do that all by himself.

Considering it was a reasonable size town, Adair was quiet when we walked in. A few houses showed the glow of oil lamps behind their curtains. Many were dark, their owners in bed. The nearby pool hall was open; so was the saloon on the main street. I could hear the occasional shouts of laughter coming from the bar. There were lights on at the station, of course. Most stations have someone waiting when a train's due, even late at night. Not that night. Surely, I thought, my nerves nagging at me, someone must see us? I still can't believe no one noticed a group of armed guys and a woman walking towards the railroad tracks from the west – and leading a horse pulling a small wagon.

The fact is, we walked in unchallenged and subdued the night telegraph operator with a couple of strong words. We also tied up a part-time station worker. Neither of them offered any resistance. While we waited for the train to come in, Grat rifled through the desk drawers in the telegraph office, and the pockets of the two employees, and came up with a few dollars. Not much but better than nothing.

Right on time, at 9:42 pm, the train steamed in sounding like a herd of restless stallions approaching mares in heat. With brakes screeching, it gasped to a stop beside us. I was nervous as hell and excited with it, but I don't think it showed. I was pretty good at keeping my feelings hidden when working by then, especially in front of the gang.

Bob and Emmett climbed up into the engine's cab with Winchesters level and ready. They captured the engineer and fireman without incident. I ran the length of the platform and persuaded the train's conductor to stay calm and do nothing – at the point of my six-gun. None of the train staff showed any inclination to start a fight. None of them wanted to argue with the spiteful end of a six-gun or a Winchester.

There were only four of us at the train at that point in the action. I don't remember seeing Newcomb, although he must have been close. Bill Doolin was with us but he didn't help much. He was too busy acting the hero: marching along the platform with a six-gun in each hand, watching the train carriages and making threatening gestures. While most of us broke into the Express car, Grat went out onto the main street and fired his guns into the night to deter any citizens from getting too curious or even brave. It wasn't the smartest thing he's ever done but it did keep him from messing up the raid in any other way.

Getting into the Express car was easy enough. Bob, me, Doolin, Newcomb and Emmett took care of that. We just blasted away at the outside in case there were any guards inside. When no lead came back at us, Bob ordered the fireman to break down the door with his pick-ax. A few minutes later we had the bank messenger opening the safe under threat of a few ounces of lead. What a disappointment. There was little real money inside. Instead of the gold bullion and cash we had expected, there were some bills, a few bankers' notes and some jewelry. It wasn't anywhere near enough to fill our wagon, though we loaded it all in anyway.

I was about to express my negative thoughts on the paucity of the haul when war broke out. Bullets began flying in all directions, mostly at us. I dived behind the wagon and hunkered down to make myself as small as possible while I figured out who was shooting at us. It didn't take long. Most of the shots were coming from the coal bunker at the end of the station's platform. From the amount of lead streaking into the night and the obvious muzzle flashes, there had to be half a dozen men at least. I heard later there were eight of them.

Eight heavily armed guards had been on that damned train and had us in their sights. They had slipped out of one of the carriages while we were breaking into the Express car and they had holed up in the coal. From there, and hidden from our view, they let fly with their Winchesters. One bullet chipped a sliver of wood off the wagon's left wheel and almost took out my eye. It was so close, I felt it shave and slit my skin as it rocketed past. It hurt like hell so I screamed. From the darkness, I heard Bob's voice.

"You okay, Flo?"

"Yeah," I answered, with a catch in my voice. "Just a scratch."

"Well keep your head down, and shuddup."

I didn't need that warning. If my head had been any lower I would have been upside down.

We blazed back at the guards and must have hit one or two of them because I heard a couple of pained yells.

Charley Pierce galloped up with our horses during a slight lull in the fight. We didn't hesitate. We mounted up and rode out of there as fast as we could, with Charley towing the horse and wagon behind him. The noise was incredible. It seemed like everyone on both sides were shooting at once, some of them at shadows. My boys were yelling with excitement. The horses were squealing and snorting in fear and the guards were shouting at us to stop. No chance of that. We were racing for the open lands beyond the town. I was scared. I was excited. I was laughing. Blood from the scratch on my face was running down to my chin. I was shooting back at the coal bunker. I must have been yelling as loud as the boys too because I had a very rough throat for the next few days.

At that point in the raid, as we raced down the main street towards safety, all we had done was to hold up a train and maybe wound a few guards. Then the night turned ugly. Predictably, it was Grat's fault. I'm convinced of that. And I was sure that Doolin was involved too. That was based on him being with Grat at the tail end of our wild ride and the number of shots fired.

There were two men sitting on chairs on the boardwalk outside Skinner's Store. Like an audience at a musical show, they were listening to the drama being acted out at the station. They suddenly had front row seats as we galloped down the middle of the street in front of them. Neither man moved, even though it should have been obvious that we were the bad guys.

Bob was in the lead, with me close behind. Emmett's horse was catching up to mine; I could see the steam from its nose off to my right. Charley Pierce, still towing the horse and wagon, was right behind. I could hear him yelling at me to get out of the way. I don't recollect the order for the rest of them. I looked behind me once to see Grat was last in line with Doolin almost beside him. Grat's nag was moving up like an express train. Why he suddenly chose to fire at the two men, other than for target practice, I could not imagine, but he did. Of course, when Bob questioned him and Doolin a week later, they both denied shooting anyone. Those denials had hollow rings to them and did not fool Bob, or me.

Bob and the gang, except me, rode into the Osage Hills to hide the night of the train raid. I didn't feel like sleeping rough. I went to the Mashed-O-Ranch instead. So it was that I got the news first, courtesy of the local paper from Adair. The two innocent citizens that Grat and possibly Doolin had shot at were front page news. They were both doctors; therefore they were important members of the community. One, Dr. Youngblood, had lost half of one of his feet. The other, Dr. Goff, had died of his wounds in the early hours of the morning after the raid.

The news report warned of five or six men, one dragging a wagon behind his horse, who had robbed the train, wounded a couple of guards and a doctor and killed poor Dr. Goff. There was no mention of a woman. I was happy about that. The really bad news was that there was now an arrest warrant out for any, or all, of the gang members. The charge would be murder. Someone had recognized at least one of the Dalton brothers. The arrest warrant named the three of them and, guessing that Doolin, Newcomb and Pierce had been involved, listed them as well.

I was so shaken up at the news that I rode out to the Guthrie hideout immediately, taking a roundabout route in case I was followed. It was just about dusk when I arrived. Bob and the boys had arrived only an hour or so before me. Bob made a smart-assed comment about me not being able to stay away from him for more than a few hours at a time. The other guys laughed and leered.

"Shut up, Bob," I groaned. "That's not even funny. Now, listen. I have bad news for you."

I showed him the newspaper and he went white.

"Jeezus," was all he said.

"There are wanted posters out for all of you in Adair, certainly in Fort Smith, probably Tulsa, Pryor Creek and everywhere else as well near here by now. The reward is five thousand dollars for each of you – dead or alive."

Bob's face went whiter. His lips tightened into thin lines and his eyes were no more than slits. He reached for his Winchester and held it by his side. Then he turned on Grat and Doolin.

"You stupid bastards," he raged. His voice was low and cold as ice. "This is all your fault. I ought to shoot the pair of you."

CHAPTER 7

For some time, Bob and the rest of the gang had been occasionally hiding out in a large cave in the granite hills outside Tulsa. We were all in the bunkhouse at the Mashed-O Ranch one morning when Bob told me he and the boys were going back to the cave as it was safer than the ranch. "And you're coming with us, Flo," he said. I looked at him in disbelief.

"You want me to live with you and these guys in a cave?" I included the rest of the gang with a theatrical wave of my hand. "Are you out of your mind? I am not living in a cave, not with you or anyone else, especially not with these animals."

"It's only for a few nights now and then," argued Bob.

"I don't care how long it is. I'm not living in a cave. Not even for thirty seconds." I was mad and it showed. Bob was getting mad, too. We stood face to face; toe to toe.

"You'll do as you're told, Flo," he shouted. "I'm the boss of this outfit and I make the decisions. We are staying in this cave for a few days. Got that?"

He reached out for my shoulders and shook me. I lost control and we were fighting again. Before he could make another move, I grabbed his arms, pulled him towards me, kneed him in the crotch and screamed, "You are not my boss and I'm not living with you in a damp and dismal cave. Understand?"

Bob was too busy on his knees, with his hands protecting his family jewels, to answer. He seemed to be having trouble breathing properly. I figured I had got my point across and prepared to leave. Emmett was watching me with his mouth wide open.

"Jesus, Flo. That wasn't necessary," he said.

"Matter of opinion, Em. I think Bob understands me now. Tell him I'll be back in a couple of days. His bruises should be down by then. Goodnight all."

I spent the next couple of nights alone in a small hotel on the outskirts of Tulsa. It was peaceful and quiet and a pleasant change of pace for me. I had a hot bath each day. I tidied up my nails. Fixed my hair and dressed like a woman again. It felt good. After three days, though, I was getting lonely and realized I missed the outdoor life, the action, and I missed Bob. I packed away my dress, put on my pants, boots and spurs and went looking. There was no way I was going to the cave. Instead I rode out to the Mashed-O and waited there. I didn't have to wait long. No more than a few hours.

I was sitting on the front porch talking with Sadie when Bob rode in alone, late in the afternoon. He stopped in front of us, sitting straight on his horse. He looked at Sadie, tipped his hat back on his head so his blond curls fell over his forehead and greeted her with a half-smile, "Afternoon, Miss Sadie."

Then he looked at me. No smile at all. Just a piercing glare from those bright blue eyes.

"I guessed you'd be here, Flo," he said. "We need to talk. I'll meet you at the bunkhouse as soon as you are ready."

He nodded once to Sadie and turned his horse away. I sat there for a while longer, not saying anything. Sadie stared into the distance. Silent. Then I stood up.

"Well," I said to Sadie with a grin. "The master has spoken. I guess I'd better go. How do I look?"

"You look just fine, Flo. He'll be waiting for you."

I sauntered over to the bunkhouse, only a couple of hundred yards away. I took it slow but kept my strides long. Bob was waiting, his hands on his hips, a mean look on his face and an unlit cigarillo hanging from his lower lip. As I got closer his expression changed; softened. I stopped a few paces away, not sure of the next move.

"Hi, Lover," I said, standing with my legs apart and my chest heaving. Okay, I admit it. I was nervous. I tugged at a strand of hair hanging over my right eye. He stepped forward; reached out one hand and pulled me to him. We didn't do a lot of talking in the bunkhouse that evening. I soon found out that Bob's private parts were back to normal. So was our relationship.

Despite the ups and downs of our love life, I didn't enjoy spending too much time away from Bob, but sometimes it was necessary. I left him for a couple of weeks in May and rode over to have a look at some stations on the Wichita to Amarillo line in southern Kansas and Oklahoma. I picked the wrong time. I was checking out the station at Harper as a possible target when storm clouds began to build over to the west. Lightning crackled and sparked at distant rocks. There was no rain but I could hear an ominous low moaning from the wind. Trouble was on its way.

CHAPTER 8

I was a long way from home and looking into the worst storm I had ever encountered. Bob and I had avoided a few small twisters the previous summer. I had never seen anything like this dangerous mess. From where I stood by the railroad tracks there was a mass of dark clouds boiling across the sky, heading from west to northwest in the early evening.

Soon after, a giant of a twister touched down and gyrated across country bent on destruction. It looked to me as though it would pass Harper to the north when it suddenly changed direction.

I mounted up and tried to outrun it but soon realized the storm would catch me and that tornado looked deadly. Instead of running, I found a depression in the southwest of town behind a new barn. That hollow was deep enough to give some shelter for me and my horse and I figured the barn might offer a bit of added protection. We settled down side by side, keeping our bodies as low to the ground as possible.

The monster storm and its violent twister ripped across the north side of Harper destroying everything in its path. Houses, businesses, a schoolhouse, a church and the tombstones in a cemetery were flattened. Outside town, farms – and the livestock on which they depended – were devastated. I heard later of two brothers who were picked up by the winds and carried about two hundred yards before being set down again. One landed without a scratch; the other was seriously injured.

I kept my head down, holding tight to my horse's neck to keep her calm, and prayed to be spared. We were lucky. The tornado left the southern half of the town untouched, venting its anger on the north side only. Once it passed, as darkness fell, I rode north to find a scene out of hell. There was little left of what had once been a thriving community. There was nothing I could do to help. Dozens of other Harper citizens were already there. I turned away to the south and vowed not to have anything to do with a raid on Harper or the surrounding area. Those folks had suffered enough for that summer.

My long ride back to the Mashed-O was a slow and sad one. I realized how fortunate I had been in finding that low land behind the barn.

When I reached the hideout, Bob was waiting to hear what I had learned. After he listened to my story, without saying a word, he thought for a while and then accepted my judgement. He nodded and said, "Okay, let's look at other possibilities on the Katy Line. I have another idea, too. I'll tell you about that one later."

CHAPTER 9

None of us really wanted to raid the Coffeeville banks. Bob's plan was so outrageous it scared us all. The general reaction was disbelief when he first presented it. Emmett spoke first, very much against it.

"Are you out of your fuckin' mind? You want us to rob both Coffeeville banks on the same day and in broad daylight? There's too many people in that town knows us, Bob. We'll never get away with it."

As I said earlier, I knew nothing about Coffeeville so I had a question for Bob. "Where's Coffeeville?"

Bob didn't answer at first. He just gave me that vicious look and pointed towards the north-east.

"Ain't you ever been to Coffeeville, Flo?" he asked. There was a lot of scorn poured into that simple question. "It's over there, a couple or more days away."

"No, Bobby," I minced the words out while wrinkling my nose at him. "I have not been to Coffeeville and I don't give a damn whether I go there or not."

We were in our hideout at the Mashed-O Ranch, just north-east of Tulsa, when Bob told us of his plans. Only a couple of days before he had said he wasn't looking at any jobs for the moment. That pronouncement sent regular gang members Bill Doolin, Bitter Creek Newcomb and Cockeye Charley Pierce off to Ingalls to look for some action there. Jim Davies had already been kicked out. So, when Bob talked about Coffeeville to the rest of us, we were all surprised.

We knew gang finances were running low. The last train robberies had yielded us a little more than $3,000. Split too many ways, it didn't amount to much for any of us, but we weren't desperate. However, money was money. So, when Bob said he had a plan for a big payday we listened.

Despite Emmett's concerns about the dangers of a double raid in daylight, Bob was adamant. We could and would rob both banks at the same time. I thought his mouth was working faster than his brain, as often happened with him, but this time I kept my mouth shut. He was in no mood to take that kind of an argument from me, or from anyone else. Even so, Emmett had another go.

"Bob, listen. If we attack both banks at the same time, that means we will be splitting our forces in two. Who's gonna watch our backs?"

Bob looked right at me, but I shook my head.

"Oh, no," I said. "I'm not getting involved in this one."

I was leaning against a wall with my thumbs hooked into my belt. I straightened up and stared back at him.

"I told you. I'm not interested in Coffeeville and I don't really care where it is."

"You'll do as you're told," Bob said as he turned back to the guys. "Now, listen, all of you. I'm not taking the whole gang. That's why I let Doolin, Newcomb and Pierce leave. We'll do this job with a smaller group."

As he talked I walked towards him. He knew I was there but he ignored me. He had a bad habit of doing that when he was pissed off with me, or trying to show the gang that he was really the boss. I walked past him. He stopped talking to watch me. I turned and faced him.

"You are not my boss," I said. "Got that, Robert Reddick Dalton? You are not my boss. If I say I'm not interested in a goddam job, I mean I'm not interested."

He started to push me aside and came face to face with the business end of my six-shooter. Everyone in the room heard the click as I cocked it.

"Jeezus!" Someone said. Nobody moved.

Bob stood there, the open end of my silver barrel touching the tip of his nose.

"Don't move, Lover," I said softly. "And don't ever push me again. You don't own me."

I released the cocking mechanism and twirled the weapon on my index finger right in front of his eyes. Bob didn't move a muscle. He knew I was right on the edge and he was in my line of fire. I glared at him for a few seconds and then, to show I still cared for him, I holstered the gun and winked at him at the same time. His eyes narrowed and I thought he was about to do something stupid when he let that dazzling smile drift across his face. I nodded, ran the tip of my tongue over my lips and gave him a ghost of a smile. Bob turned to one side to avoid looking at me and faced the guys. He shook his head.

"Fuckin' women," he said; his voice just a little hoarse and a mite shaky. "Okay, now everyone listen. You too, if you want to, Flo."

THE SIXTH MAN

I had taken just about enough of his crap. I stood in front of him and said, "I told you, Bob Dalton. I am not going to Coffeeville and I still don't give a damn where it is."

Bob lost his temper and slapped me. I slapped him in return. I heard a voice from behind me say, "Oh, shit. Now she's done it."

Bob put one hand up to his face, his eyes narrowed. "You bitch," he snarled and slapped me again. That one rocked me a bit but I stayed upright and hit him as hard as I could with my open hand. He didn't hit me back, oh no, instead he drew a gun on me. I could see he was mad enough to pull the trigger so I took a couple of paces back.

"Flo… ," he started, his voice rasping with anger, his hand shaking and the barrel of his six-gun waving in my direction. I didn't let him finish. I backed up some more. My whip lashed out, curled tight round his ankles and I heaved back with all my might. Bob went down in a heap; his gun went off and put a bullet through the ceiling.

"Nice shot, Bob," I said as I started to untie his legs. "You missed."

The guys stood there with their mouths open in shock, although Emmett had a ghost of a smile flickering around his mouth.

Bob reached up and grabbed my shirt. Before I could wriggle free he had me down on top of him full length and suddenly everything changed. I could feel his lean, hard body under me and he had my much softer and curvier body draped over him. We both burst out laughing. Forgetting we were being watched, Bob rolled me over onto my back and started to undo my shirt.

"Uh, Bob," I said, "We do have an audience, you know."

Bob looked up to see a row of stupid grins. He shook his head and stood up, pulling me to my feet. Grat leered at him and asked, "Ain't ya gonna…?"

Bob cut him off with a curt, "Shuddup, Grat, or I'll flatten you."

Grat started to argue but Emmett stopped him with a hand over his mouth. "Enough questions, Grat," he said. "Now, Bob, tell us your plans."

Bob lit a smoke, taking his time. I could see he was waiting for the gang to pay attention. At last he pointed to each of his brothers and the three remaining members of the gang in turn as he called the names, "There'll be just me, Emmett and Grat, plus you Dick Broadwell, and you Bill Powers, and, of course, Flo."

I started to argue, so did Emmett. Bob cut us off.

"Emmett, you and me, we'll hit the First National while Grat, Bill and Dick crack the Condon Bank."

"What about me? Where am I supposed to be?" I didn't want to go but, if I had to be with them, I needed a job.

Bob lost his temper again and yelled at me. "I thought you weren't interested, Flo. Make up your damned mind, woman. Okay. You want a job? You'll be looking after the mounts, and watching out for us. Now shuddup a minute while I explain. I've had just about enough of your lip for one day."

No one tells me to shut up and gets away with it.

"You can kiss my a…," I started to swear at him but stopped halfway through the thought. Bob's eyes were smoldering. His lips stretched into thin parallel lines. He pointed a finger at me and said one shaky word, "Flo." It was enough. His look did the rest. I changed my mind and did as I was told. Picking another fight with him when he was laying out plans made no sense at all. That would just put him into a blacker mood and that could be dangerous in front of the men. My annoyance would keep for later, when we were alone. Then I'd make him suffer.

"Bob, this ain't a good idea," Emmet diffused the moment by trying to reason with him. "There's folks in Coffeeville knows us too well. Somebody's sure to recognize us. Even the James boys wouldn't try this one. I don't think I want any part of it, and that's a fact."

"Forget the James boys. We're better than them. We can and we will hit both banks at the same time. No one in town will expect that. Trust me. I know what I'm doing."

Bob glared at each one of us in turn, daring anyone to contradict him. Emmett backed off, but I could see he wasn't happy. Neither was I. Coffeyville, Emmett explained to me, was about sixty miles almost due north of our hideout.

We could have been there in a couple of days but Bob decided we'd take close to two weeks to ride up there. That was hard on the nerves: just riding a handful of miles each day, always wondering and waiting to see if the raid would really happen. We stopped regularly, sometimes for a few days at a time. I began to wonder if Bob was having second thoughts about the job.

We stayed for a few days at a spread beside Candy Creek. Bob and Emmett knew the owners somehow but I never saw them the whole time we were there. I think he said they'd gone to Tulsa for a few days. There the horses had a rest while Bob went over the plans with us. I listened but continued to have my doubts about the robbery. It just did not sound like a good idea to me. I tried to talk to Bob about it in bed that night, but he wouldn't listen.

"Flo, Flo, Flo," he groaned. "You're supposed to be on my side. What's got in to you?"

"I'm just saying, Bob, I think hitting two banks at once is a real bad idea: especially in broad daylight. There'll be people on the street, on the sidewalks and in the banks. Someone's gonna get shot for sure."

Bob got out of bed and stamped out onto the porch for a smoke. He was mad at me for disagreeing with him and I was mad at him for not listening to reason. When he came back to bed I pretended to be asleep. He reached for me anyway.

"Get your hands off me, Bob Dalton," I said quietly, "or I'll blow your cock off, and not in the way you like."

He knew I wasn't kidding when he felt the hard steel of my Colt up against his privates.

"Jeez, Flo. What the hell's the matter with you? What are you trying to do?" his voice climbed high and his manhood fell down.

"Just keep your hands to yourself. I'm not interested." I was but I sure wasn't going to admit it right then. Bob turned away from me muttering something unpleasant about women and the moon. I ignored him, stuck the gun under my pillow and went to sleep for a while. I kept waking up though, wondering if Bob was awake. He wasn't snoring. He was very quiet. We stayed like that for a few hours, Bob on the left side of the bed and me on the right; our backs staring at each other without touching. Eventually we both gave up the pretense and merged into one, as we did most mornings.

We stopped again at a homestead a couple of days after leaving Candy Creek. Bob told me to button my shirt up properly as the owners were old friends of the Dalton family. I didn't see what difference that made but did as I was told for a change anyway. The homesteaders were happy to see the Dalton boys. Bob was obviously a special favorite so he got the lion's share of the good treatment. I was introduced as Bob's lady friend and soon accepted as one of the family.

The husband's name was Claude, and his wife was Peggy. I think their last name was Simmonds, or Timmons, or something like that. Anyway, they had a teenage son, Clay, no more than fourteen I guessed. He couldn't keep his eyes off me, especially where my shirt pushed out in front. I smiled at him one morning and suggested he let me help him around the spread while Bob and the boys chatted about old times with Claude and Peggy. Claude thought getting me to help was a good idea.

"Take Flo out to the hollow," he suggested. "There's a couple or more of fence posts needs straightening out there, else they'll be down next time we get any wind."

We rode out along a shallow creek for a half a mile or so into some scrubland, where the ground dipped for a while. There, out of sight of the house, were five posts needing serious attention. One was already on the ground.

"I guess this is the place," I said as I dismounted. I had undone the top three buttons of my shirt as soon as we left the house. I scratched lightly at the swell of my chest as I was talking. Clay's eyes almost popped out of his young head. His hormones were on fire and his blood was overheating. He stood beside his horse with a bulge building in his britches that suggested he might become a real man someday soon. I wondered if, maybe, I should help him on his way. I smiled at him and he grinned at me, his face redder than it had been a few minutes before.

"You got something on your mind, Clay?" I asked, quietly, looking from his eyes to his bulge. "Are you planning to use that thing on me?"

"No. No, ma'am," he began to stutter. "No, ma'am. Nothin' like that."

"Well, now, Clay, I don't know whether to be disappointed or insulted. Don't you like me?" I was purring like a kitten. Looking him straight in the eyes, I reached out with one finger to touch his bulge, which looked like it was about to break out of hiding. Clay jumped and took a step back as the top of my finger stroked him. I took a step forward and touched him again. It didn't take long after that. Not long at all.

"Whoa, Clay," I crooned. "You're supposed to wait for me."

"I, I'm s-s-sorry, ma'am. I'm sorry," Clay's face had gone scarlet and he was almost in tears.

"That's okay," I whispered, holding him in my arms. "Let's see if we can start again, shall we?"

I pulled him down to the ground and stretched out on my back. He was a quick learner. I'll say that for him. Young Clay became a man that day, with a little help from me, and this time we both enjoyed it. With that business taken care of, we worked together to repair the fence posts and then managed to get Clay's blood pressure up again. By the time we rode in for supper he was one tired young man and ready for a good night's sleep – all by himself.

At supper time that night Peggy bustled between the hot stove and the dining table. I helped her but kept my ears on the conversation going on close by.

"So, where you boys heading for next, Bob?" Claude asked.

Before Bob got his mouth working I had mine open and about to get me in trouble.

"We're going to Coffeeville for a couple of days. I've never been there. Have you, Peggy?"

You should have seen Bob's face. I knew I'd spoken out of turn but it was too late to take the words back. Fortunately for me, Grat interrupted before Bob could say a word.

"Yep, that's right," he crowed, "we're goin' to Coffeeville all right. Got us some banking to do."

Well, you should have heard the sudden silence. It was like a storm cloud ready to let loose prairie thunder and lightning and rain all at once. Nobody moved. They just sat there like they were in a picture. Claude looked surprised. Clay was too busy looking at me. Emmett was watching Bob out the corners of his eyes. Peggy didn't seem to notice anything had happened. Perhaps she hadn't heard what Grat said. She just carried on serving up the food. I shut up and stared at the men, expecting the worst. Bob and the other guys were giving Grat the evil eye and Bob was trying to say "Shut the fuck up" without moving his lips. Grat didn't get it. He was the only one who moved. He looked from Bob to Emmett and back again.

"What?" he asked. "What have I done now?"

Peggy got the evening back on track and the picture in motion again with a cheerful, "Enough talk now, boys. Eat while it's hot."

Bob looked over to Claude. "We're only staying a couple of days up there in Coffeeville. I have some people I want to see about some work this winter and, as Grat said, there's some money to put in the bank for safety."

I happened to look at Grat as Bob spoke and could see the confusion on his face. Before anyone could stop him, he said, "Put money in the bank? I thought we was gonna take it out."

If anyone had lit a match near Bob at that moment he would have exploded. He turned slowly to look at Grat, three seats to his left. Bob's face was white. His eyes were no more than slits, so narrow I doubt anyone could even see the blue. His lips were bloodless lines.

"Grat," he said, his voice harsh, like he was trying not to cough, "pass me the potatoes, will you?"

Grat reached for the bowl and handed it down to Bob. He was still looking confused. "Yeah, but, Bob," he started.

Bob cut him off with, "Don't talk with your mouth full. It's rude."

"Yeah, but…"

Before Grat could say anything else, Emmett, who was sitting at the end of the table nearest Grat, reached over and shook his shoulder. "Shut up and eat your supper, Grat. We don't want Miss Peggy's good cooking to get cold now, do we?"

Grat kept quiet throughout the rest of the meal. He was too busy stuffing his mouth to get into any more trouble. I chatted with Peggy while Bob talked farming with Claude. Although his conversation sounded relaxed, I could sense the tension in Bob and knew he was seething inside.

We left at sunup next morning. As we finished our coffee and thanked Peggy for her hospitality, Bob pressed a twenty-dollar gold piece into Peggy's hand.

"Take it," he ordered, "with our thanks. No argument now."

Peggy nodded and kissed him on the side of his face. "Thanks, Bob," she said. "We can sure use this right now, although, God knows, I don't like to take money from family."

Bob nodded and touched her cheek. "I know," he said softly. "I know."

"Now you all behave yourselves up there in Coffeeville, you hear?" Peggy called as we mounted up.

Grat grinned and started to say, "Oh, we're gonna have some fu…" He stopped when he saw the look on Bob's face. Murder was written right across it. "Oh, right," Grat finished and shook his head. He still looked confused to me.

We rode out with Bob in the lead and me half a pace behind him to his right. Over by the barn, Claude was fixing a fence post. Clay was out ploughing a field, carving a straight furrow behind a sturdy old horse. They both stopped work briefly, took off their hats and waved. I waved back at both, but my eyes were on Clay. Despite the work he had to get done that day, all of it exhausting, he grinned and waved his hat once more for me.

"Nice family," I said to Bob as we headed north.

"They sure are. My ma knew Peggy's folks real well many years ago."

We rode in silence for a while after that. It's just as well that I was slightly behind Bob and off to one side so, unless he looked back, he couldn't see the stupid grin on my face.

Bob stopped an hour beyond the farm. Without saying a word to anyone, he handed me the reins to his horse and walked the few paces back towards the others. He stopped beside Grat and said quietly, "Get down, Grat."

Grat looked at Bob, then at me, to Emmett and back to Bob again.

"What have I done?" he asked.

"Just get down, Grat."

Suddenly, it was like a light had come on in Grat's brain. We could all see the look of recognition on his face. Fast as a striking rattler, he had his six-gun in his hand and pointing at Bob. But Bob was no longer there. He had ducked under Grat's horse. He came up the other side and dragged his brother off in one smooth movement.

They fought with their fists for what seemed like hours. As brothers, they were much the same size. As brawlers, they were also evenly matched, except that Bob was real angry and Grat knew it; that made him nervous and a little careless. The fight ended when Bob kicked Grat in the crotch and then knocked him cold with a mighty uppercut to the jaw. Both men had bloodied fists and faces.

Bob ignored his own pains and threw water on Grat's face to wake him up. He walked to me, took the reins from my hand, mounted up and said, "Let's go."

When I looked back, Emmett was helping Grat onto his horse. They followed us without another word.

Clouds were rolling in from the west by mid-morning and it was obvious we were going to get wet. I mentioned the probability to Bob.

"Yeah. Looks like it, don't it? A good rain'll soon cover our tracks and that's okay by me."

We got a good rain all right. Even with my poncho on, I couldn't have got any wetter if I'd fallen in a flooded creek fully clothed. We made camp that night out in the open. The rain had eased off to a light drizzle but the

THE SIXTH MAN

ground was soaked. It was not a comfortable night for any of us.

There was a bit of frost next morning. I woke up cold, wet and tired, but glad to see the daylight. I heated up some bacon and beans while Bob brewed a pot of coffee.

"How far you fixin' to travel today, Bob?" Emmett asked.

"Onion Creek. It's not far. We'll stop there for tonight and go on to Coffeeville tomorrow."

I'd never heard of Onion Creek but said nothing, for a change. Wherever it was, it was one stage closer to the banks. We took our time over breakfast and then, after a last drag on his smoke, Bob stood up. "Let's go," he said as he kicked dirt over the fire to put it out. I poured the rest of the coffee over it. We got up, stretched, and saddled our horses. After stowing the pots, pans and tin cups in our saddlebags, one by one we mounted up and followed Bob towards our destination.

That day we rode even slower than we had on the other days, letting the horses take as much time as they wanted. We knew we would need them to be strong later and we'd need them to be fresh. No point in wearing them out now.

We stopped to rest the horses and stretch our own legs among the shade trees beside Hickory Creek in the late afternoon. As soon as it got dark we moved on a short distance to camp beside a dry river bed. Bob said it was Onion Creek. I wondered how it got its name, even asked the question, but none of the gang knew the answer.

"It's just a name, Flo. It's Onion Creek. Just a name," Bob sounded pissed off with me so I shut up for a while.

It was cold again that night, but dry. After an equally cold dinner of hard-boiled eggs and even harder biscuits, we tried to sleep. I cuddled up under a blanket behind Bob to keep warm but he was restless and so was I so neither of us got much shut-eye.

When I pushed my blanket aside and stood up, the date was Wednesday, October 5, 1892. That's one date I'll never forget. It was actually a nice morning, apart from being a bit frosty at dawn. I thought it showed promise of growing into a beautiful autumn day, although I don't think the boys even noticed.

At first, Bob was real quiet while we were getting ready to leave. He just sat by himself, smoking and thinking, with his Winchester across his knees. Emmett was quiet too for a while. Grat wasn't. He must have eaten a lot more eggs than the rest of us, and more beans the previous day because he farted loudly every few minutes and laughed out loud each time. Broadwell and Powers joked about the smell but Bob was not amused. At one point, he said in his dangerous, quiet voice, "Stick a cork in it, Grat. Or I'll plug it with this." He tapped the rifle for emphasis.

Grat wandered away singing to himself, "Wherever you be let your wind go free." He farted with every other step. It would have been funny at any other time but that morning was serious, only Grat, being stupid, couldn't figure that out.

I was sitting by myself staring at some ice on a puddle of water. Part of the ice looked like a star. I wondered if it was a good omen. I hoped so. I was so scared that morning, I was almost in tears.

Bob came over and stood in front of me. "What's the matter, Flo?" He asked.

I looked up at him. "I'm scared, Bob. I'm scared."

"There's nothing to be scared of. It's just another job."

I sniffed and wiped away a tear. "I'm scared of losing you, Bob," I said quietly.

He stepped forward and squatted in front of me. "You're not gonna lose me, Flo. We're in this together, all the way. Nothing bad's gonna happen to me. Now come on, let's get ready to ride."

As he straightened up and walked away I noticed his right boot had crushed the star, leaving a different, much uglier picture. Now it looked like a laughing skull. I shivered and wiped the image away with the toe of my boot as I stood. At that moment, I knew it was a bad omen, but I knew Bob would not want to hear about it. He was already making final preparations for the day and giving out orders.

"Check your weapons before we leave, everyone," Bob ordered. "Today will be like no other. No one's ever tried to pull off a heist like this one. By this afternoon we'll all be rich and we'll all be famous."

Yeah. Maybe we'll all be dead, too, I thought.

CHAPTER 10

As we were getting ready to mount up I was resigned to whatever the day would bring. By then, Bob's thoughtful mood had passed. He and Emmett were soon showing high spirits and clowning around with each other like excited boys. I was worried as hell, but they acted like they didn't have a care in the world.

"On to Coffeeville, boys. This is our last trick," Bob shouted and laughed. Emmett laughed with him and punched his brother's shoulder. The two circled each other with their fists up, like two boxers looking for an opening, but they were both laughing. Bob was wearing a long coat. Emmett teased him about it.

"You won't need that coat when we get to town, Bob. It's gonna be hot enough up there for sure."

They shook hands and laughed again. Grat, Bill, and Dick each took a long slug of Dutch courage, wiped their mouths and joined in the fun. Grat offered Bob a pull at the bottle of white lightning but he shook his head with a smile.

"No. I don't need that. I'm ready."

Emmett accepted the bottle, took a quick gulp and handed it back.

"Me too," he agreed.

No one thought to offer me a drink. I didn't need it either, but it would have been nice to be asked.

Bob wrapped a scarf around his neck, pulled his coat collar up and bent to check all four hooves on his horse.

"Make sure all the horses are in good shape," he called. "We can't afford any of them to go lame on us."

I'd checked my horse the night before, but I checked again anyway. The fetlocks and hooves were fine. Shoes in place and tight, and no stones to be seen. After tucking my long hair down inside the back of my coat and tilting my Stetson forward over my eyes, I was ready. Bob took one last look around our little campsite, winked at me and then turned to his horse.

"Okay," he said, as he mounted up, "let's go to Coffeeville."

That slow, early morning ride into town from our last camp seemed to take forever. There were a few interruptions, of course. There always were. As we came out of Onion Creek we passed a young girl riding towards town. She looked at us but made no comment.

Silliest part of the morning, as far as I was concerned, was when Bob put on false whiskers a few minutes later.

"What the hell are you doing that for?" I asked. "Now you look ridiculous."

"It's a disguise, Flo. Just a simple disguise," he ranted. "We're all wearing them."

I looked back. He was right. Each member of the gang, except me, was wearing false whiskers. God, they looked stupid and real phony. Nervous as I was at the job we were heading for, I could see the funny side of the situation. I started to laugh. That got Bob mad.

"What the hell are you laughing at now, Flo?" he asked. "What's so funny?"

"You all look so stupid. Those whiskers won't fool anyone." I started laughing again, but I moved my horse away from his so he couldn't swing his fist out and hit me.

"Damn you, Flo," he said, but he pulled off the whiskers anyway and tucked them into his shirt. The other guys kept their disguises on. They still looked stupid. Bob didn't.

As we rode along I was thinking about the guns the boys carried. Bob had his Winchester, of course. He never went anywhere without it, unless it was to bed with me; even then he kept it close at hand. He also had his usual six-shooter on his hip, plus a Colt .44 in his right boot, and a small, British made .38 tucked inside his vest. The others were similarly armed, although I think they only carried a Winchester each and two six-shooters. I had my own Winchester, my six-shooter and my trusty whip. We each had about a hundred or more rounds of ammo. I guess you could say we were well armed for the raid. For some reason, that didn't comfort me as much as it should have.

Bob rode in silence after he took off the whiskers. His back was straight and he never looked to right or left. I could tell he was mad at me but he was also thinking through all the moves. His plan, as we all knew, was to tie the horses to the hitching rail outside McCoy's Hardware store, on the corner of 8th Street and Walnut Street about 9:30 in the morning. The timing was important. We had to be at the banks before there could be too many substantial withdrawals. That hitching rail, he said, was just one short block from the Condon Bank. I was to wait there, looking innocent, and watch the horses. Because Bob had refused to allow Emmett, or anyone else for that matter, to go into town a few days earlier and make sure everything was as he remembered it, nothing would work out the way it should have, but we didn't know that, yet.

We rode past a herd of sheep. Grat and Powers started to "baaa" at them and then burst out laughing. Bob looked back and shook his head in annoyance.

"Grat, shut the fuck up, will ya?" he called. "You and Emmett, ride on up here with me. Flo, you stay back a bit. Powers and Broadwell, you guys bring up the rear. And everyone, shuddup."

We changed the formation as ordered and rode on. No more talking now. The three brothers, with Bob in the middle, could easily have passed for a law posse coming in from the Indian Territory, if Grat and Emmett hadn't been wearing those stupid whiskers.

About a mile west of Coffeeville, where a dairy farm stood, we turned towards town. We passed a buckboard with a man and a woman on board going in the opposite direction. I remember Bob tipped his hat to the lady as they passed and the man beside her responded the same way. Polite and instinctive on both sides, it seemed to me. Soon after, we passed a couple more good citizens going about their morning business. Those two looked at us more closely. I reckon it was the whiskers that made them curious, but they didn't stop or talk to us. They just rode on out of town, though one of them looked back, just as I was looking back at them. I spurred my horse and caught up with the brothers.

"Bob," I said, "One of those guys we just passed recognized you, I think. Either that or he is worried about the false whiskers."

"Is he following us?" Bob asked without turning.

I looked back. "No."

"Then pay him no mind, Flo."

"Pay him no mind, Flo," I mimicked as I dropped back a few paces. "Pay him no mind, Flo."

On the edge of town, the west side, the dusty trail we were following became a real street. It wasn't paved of course, not in those days, but it was known as 8th Street. When we reached the white Episcopalian Church, on the corner of 8th and Maple Streets, we turned south and rode slowly past the big warehouse of the Long-Bell Lumber Company.

I looked around me with a sense of wonder at the many red-brick buildings. Coffeeville just looked so damn rich. I'd never seen anyplace like that town. It looked even better than Tulsa to me. Bob interrupted my thoughts as we approached the corner of Walnut and 8th Streets.

"Damn. The hitchin' rail's gone from McCoy's. The street's all tore up," he complained. "Turn back. We gotta find somewhere else, maybe down the next alley."

We pulled our horses around with as little fuss as we could and followed Bob onto 8th Street and down a narrow side street to a back alley.

"This will do," he said. "We'll leave the horse here. Flo, you look after them."

I think Bob Dalton was nervous for the first time in his life that Kansas morning. As I got off my horse in the alley, he put one arm around my waist and held me tight. He looked me in the eyes, smiled, and kissed me.

"You take care of yourself, Bob Dalton, please," I begged, searching his beautiful blue eyes for something I couldn't see. Then, for the first and only time, I admitted in almost a whisper, "I love you."

"Yeah," he drawled the word into one long exhaled breath and turned away, the muzzle of his Winchester pointed at the ground. Without looking back, he said, "We'll be out again before you know it. Be ready for us, Flo. We'll probably be in a hurry."

With that, Bob Dalton walked away and out of my life forever, although I didn't know then that I would never hold him again. I was so scared. I could not see any way this raid could possibly work without bloodshed. Emmett walked a few paces behind Bob, his Winchester pointing at the ground. Neither of them seemed to be in a hurry. The day seemed to have gone into slow motion.

The others, Grat, Bill and Dick, handed me their reins, pulled their Winchesters out of their saddle-boots and followed the boss. They weren't walking any faster. I think they were all scared by that time, except perhaps for Grat. He was too stupid to be scared of anything.

As I said, I was scared. I was scared enough for all of them, and I don't scare easily. I just had a sick feeling in the pit of my stomach that something was about to go horribly wrong. I almost cried out to Bob to come back, but I didn't. I wish I had. Oh, God, I wish I had.

CHAPTER 11

Bob had told me to stay with the horses. I was never happy with that idea. I couldn't imagine standing there waiting and wondering what was happening to my boys. As the gang strode along the alley to Walnut Street and disappeared out of sight, I made a quick decision. My boys were gonna need back up and I was just the woman to look after them. I looped all the reins over a fence and followed. I didn't know it at the time, but that fence was on a judge's property.

From just inside the alley, I saw Bob and Emmett cross Walnut Street, passing the red brick front of Condon's Bank, and continue across the bottom of Union Street. I noticed that Bob looked around him as they crossed the street: from left to right and from right to left, walking straight towards the smaller, wood framed First National Bank.

Grat and the other two were half a dozen paces behind. They had just walked out onto Walnut Street when a young man driving a wagon turned into the alley, coming straight at me. I had to flatten myself against a fence to let the two horses and wagon past. The young driver, not much more than a boy really, raised his hat to me and said, "Howdy, ma'am. Sorry to be in the way."

I rewarded his courtesy with a smile, thinking he was in the way all right. Our horses were in his way, too.

"Do you want me to move those horses?" I asked. "One of them's mine."

"No, ma'am," he answered. "I'm not going that far. I have a delivery at Slosson's right here." He stopped the wagon and climbed down, giving me a cheeky grin as he did so, his eyes on my chest, instead of my face.

Normally I would have had a come-back for him but that morning I was far too tense to respond with my usual style. Thanks to him, I had lost sight of my boys. I was worried. Bob and Emmett would surely have entered their bank by then and Grat's trio should have been in the Condon.

The street was busy. There were a few people on the sidewalks and a number of rigs parked on the sides of the road, their horses waiting in practiced boredom. I saw a man wearing a cloth apron over his business clothes standing on the sidewalk outside McKenna and Adamson's Dry Good Store, to the left of the alley from me. He had a broom in his hands and was looking straight at the Condon Bank with a surprised look on his face. From where I stood, no more than three long strides away from him, I could see clear through the window of Condon's Bank. There, for anyone else to see as well, was Grat Dalton with his Winchester up at his shoulder, pointed at a bank teller who had his arms in the air. The man saw Grat at the same time. He immediately looked across at the First National, where Bob and Emmett had gone. He must have seen them, armed to the teeth, walking across the street a few minutes earlier. It didn't take him long to put two and three together and come up with five. Before I could take a shot at him, he dropped his broom and ran into the dry goods store, yelling his head off.

"The Dalton gang's here and they're robbing our banks."

"Shit!" I exploded as I watched the plan beginning to disintegrate. I placed one foot forward to run across to warn Bob but it was already too late. Word of the robberies in progress spread like a wild-fire. The man with the apron came out of his store with a shotgun in his hands. I did a quick about turn and put myself back in the alley. From there, I figured, with a bit of luck, I could cover the boys as they came out of the banks.

Unknown to me at the time, although I guessed it must be happening, the alarmed citizens of Coffeeville were arming themselves to do battle with the robbers. All I could do was to watch and wait, and try to help my boys. I looked back down the alley. That damned wagon was still there behind Slosson's; beyond it I could just see our horses.

I stood against a wall, trying to be inconspicuous and probably failing. My Winchester and my whip were on my horse but I still had my six-shooter, and my Bowie knife in my boot. I knew I could do a lot of damage with each one of them. The Winchester, though, was the most important. I couldn't see what was happening inside the First National and not much at Condon's either.

"C'mon, you guys. Come on!" In desperation, I spoke out loud, almost a prayer. My feet were dancing with impatience and barely controlled fear. *I've gotta get that rifle.* The thought pushed me like an order.

I squeezed past the wagon and ran back to my horse. I pulled the Winchester out of its saddle holster but left my whip. Already I was too late; I knew that. Even so, I ran back along the alley, past the two horses and wagon, as the first shots echoed across town. When I reached the corner of the alley and Walnut Street, the center of Coffeeville was a battlefield. I raised my rifle and took a shot at someone with a carbine close to Condon's bank. Seeing a lot of other citizens with guns on the streets, behind wooden barrels and in doorways, I knew there was nothing else I could do to help near the banks. I had to get the horses ready and I had to do it fast. I let off a couple of shots, random but noisy, then ran for the horses.

That damned wagon was still in the alley behind Slosson's, with the wide-eyed young driver crouching beside it.

"You okay, ma'am?" He called to me as I ran past.

"Yeah," I shouted back. "You'd better get the heck outta here. Can't you see there's a war going on? Take your wagon and go. Now! Go!"

I sprinted the rest of the way to our horses, took their reins and held them out of the way so the wagon could roll past, when the kid finally got his horses moving. Then, when the boys came out of the banks with the money, I would be ready for them. I would mount my horse and lead the others at a gallop to meet them. That was my plan, pure and simple. Too bad it didn't turn out that way.

The kid ignored my warning and ran back into Slosson's. The wagon was stationary, and that meant I did not have a clear run along the alley to the street, unless I took the horses in single file. That would take far too long.

While I was in the alley, the action was heating up across the street. Most of what I learned about the events in the banks came from a long story in the Coffeeville Journal soon after the raid. The rest came from Emmett a couple of years later. I visited him in the jail at Lansing, Kansas, where he was serving a life sentence for his part in the killings in Coffeeville. I had to pose as his sister to get in but it was worth it. I had to talk about Bob with someone who knew him well, just so I could let him go, finally, and get on with my life.

Emmett's story was not a pretty one. In fact, it was a tale of disaster and Bob Dalton, leader of the gang and my lover, was to blame for faulty planning. I already knew that. I wanted more details about what happened in the banks. Emmett confirmed that he and Bob almost got away with their part of the raid. Nothing went wrong in the First National Bank. They lifted $20,000 or more from the tellers and the vault without having to fire any shots or any other vilence. It was over at Condon's Bank where things went haywire.

If it hadn't been for Grat, Bob would be alive today. I really believe that. With a little help from Broadwell and Powers, Grat turned the raid into a farce. I'm convinced that Grat Dalton and his pathetic little mind can be blamed for getting Bob killed.

Of course, looking at it from another point of view, and with the advantage of hindsight, if it hadn't been so serious, parts of the raid would have been downright hilarious. Even now, when I think of Grat's juvenile performance as I heard about it, I have to shake my head in wonder and, yes, even smile a little at his incredible stupidity.

THE SIXTH MAN

Picture this: Grat Dalton, Dick Broadwell and Bill Powers march into Condon's Bank, three sets of spurs jingling and three loaded Winchesters ready for use. Broadwell guards the opposite door while Grat unleashes his repertoire of profanity on one of the tellers. "Get your fuckin' hands up."

As the teller puts his hands up, a customer walks in through the main door. About the same time, the head cashier comes out of his office wondering what the shouting is about. He and the customer find themselves staring at the business ends of a trio of Winchesters.

"Down on the floor. Down on the fuckin' floor, now," shouts Grat to the customer. To the cashier, he yells, "You. Hold this open and you…" he points his Winchester at the teller, "You fill it up with every damned dollar you've got in here."

Another customer opens the front door, looks in, sees the danger, and quickly closes the door, from the outside. Grat and the other two villains must have seen him, or heard him, yet they ignore the interruption. Grat sees the door to the vault is open.

"You two," he aims his rifle at the bankers, "open the safe in there."

Charles Ball, the cashier, glances at his pocket watch and says, "Can't do that. There's a timer on the lock. It will open automatically at 9:30."

That took guts because it was a blatant lie as Grat would have known if he'd just looked to his right. According to the story, there was a clock on the wall there, in full view, which declared to the time to be somewhat later than 9:30. The clock showed 9:40, or something close. Grat, not even aware of the clock, asks Ball, "What's the fuckin' time now?"

78

Charles Ball had some sand, you gotta say that for him. He looks Grat right in the eye and says, "Another ten minutes before it opens."

And Grat believes him. "Okay," he says, "we'll wait."

Can you imagine it? Three armed robbers in a bank prepared to wait ten minutes for a time lock to open. Only Grat Dalton could have written a scene like that. The gang didn't wait ten minutes, of course. Even Grat wasn't quite that stupid. After a couple of minutes staring at the safe door, Grat starts to get mad.

He screams at Ball, "You're lying to me, you bastard. I know you're fuckin' well lying. Now open this fuckin' door and give us all the money and the gold."

By this time his voice is about as loud as it can get and he's waving a loaded Winchester at the banker. It doesn't faze Charles Ball one bit. He stands there, in extreme danger, and tells another lie with a straight face.

"There isn't any money or gold in there," he explains. "We're waiting for a delivery any day now. You've already taken all the cash we have."

Predictably, Grat goes berserk, screaming abuse at the bankers and waving his Winchester all over the place. Broadwell and Powers just stand there and watch, looking from Grat's angry red face to the white faces of the bankers and back. Neither of them thinks to take a look out the windows to see if anyone outside has heard the commotion.

Fact is, the armed gang had been seen going into the banks and the good citizens of Coffeeville were grabbing firearms and getting ready for a fight to save their money. Grat's temper had distracted Broadwell and Powers from keeping watch. They were about to learn that trouble was all around them.

Meanwhile, across the road at the First National Bank, that robbery was unfolding with its own drama for Bob and Emmett. With masks covering their faces and Winchesters at the ready, the brothers exploded into the bank to find three customers and three bank employees. None were obviously armed. Then another good citizen opened the door. Emmett dragged him in and pushed him over to the other customers. While Emmett kept control of the customers and a couple of clerks, Bob marched behind the counter and into the back of the bank. Bert Ayres, a young man who knew Bob Dalton, sat at a desk. He was the bank's book keeper. His father, Tom, was one of the clerks being threatened by Emmett's rifle.

"Open the vault, now, Bert," Bob yelled at the younger Ayres.

Bert Ayres just sat there and shook his head. "I can't," he lied. "I don't have the combination."

"Tom Ayres," Bob Dalton shouted. "Come here and open this damned vault."

Tom did as he was told and handed Bob a small sack with money in it. He added the contents of the cashier's till. Bob looked around him, then back at Tom.

"Is this all the money in the bank?"

Before Tom Ayres could lie, the cashier blurted out, "No, there's some gold and silver in the vault."

Bob swung round, his Winchester aimed at Tom Ayres. "Go get it, Tom." His voice was quiet and deadly. Tom did as he was told, coming back with another small sack. Bob pushed past him in disbelief and looked in the vault for himself. He came back out with a couple more small sacks – both full.

"Time to go, Em," he said. Then, to the customers and bank staff, "Outside now, all of you, in front of us to the street."

As Bob and Emmett cleared the bank's front door, a couple of bullets slammed into the wall behind them. They ran back into the bank followed by Bert Ayres and one of the customers.

"Look after the money, Em," Bob ordered. "I'll hold them off."

Bob let fly a few rounds and, being the best damned shot in the territory, he probably did some serious damage to anyone in his sights.

Meanwhile, across Union Street, bullets suddenly started flying into Condon's from Walnut Street. Broadwell fired back and the battle was on. Grat turned to Charles Ball with a question and was met with another lie. It went like this:

Grat: "Is there a back door to this bank?"

Ball: "No."

And Grat believed him. There was a back door and if Grat, Powers, or Broadwell had had the sense to go and look, they would have seen it.

"Fuck it," Grat let rip. "We'll go out the front, the way we came in."

He motioned the two bankers to carry the sack of money, planning to use them as cover to get across the wide space where Union and Walnut Streets met to reach the alley. The citizens' army had other ideas. They bombarded the bank with rifle and pistol fire, making it impossible for the gang to leave. The three outlaws and the bankers hit the floor for safety. Broadwell raised himself up and took a shot out the window and received a bullet in his arm and another in his body as he fell.

Neither wound was fatal but they would have been very painful.

Grat now decided to try and leave again, despite the danger. He thrust his hands into the money bag and stuffed his shirt with bank notes, then yelled at Broadwell and Powers, "Come on. We gotta get outta here."

With their guns firing, he and Powers raced out the door and ran through the storm of bullets towards the alley. Dick Broadwell staggered along behind them, trailing blood but still shooting.

Bob and Emmett ran out the back door of the First National, turned left and raced the length of a back alley to 8th Street. There they slowed, turned left again and sauntered to the corner of Union Street.

I was just inside the alley, watching and waiting. I saw Grat and his partners come out of Condon's Bank and gave them covering fire as much as I could, but then I had to retreat for my own safety. Bob and Emmett did their bit too. They opened up with their Winchesters from the corner of Union and 8th Street to give covering cross-fire; enough so that the other three could reach the alley.

About that time it became really confusing. I was in the alley releasing the horses and turning them ready for flight. As far as I recall, Emmett and Bob reached the alley unhurt. They were followed soon after by Grat and Powers. Both had obviously been hit but were still on the feet and blazing away at the townsfolk. Bob and Emmett covered them from the middle of the alley.

I watched in horror as Bob took a direct hit and crumbled off to one side. I didn't know if he was alive or dead – but he didn't move. Emmett went down next and then Grat. Seconds later Bill Powers dropped close by. Next thing I saw was Broadwell hobbling down the alley as fast as he could, yelling at me, "Git outta here. Git outta here. They're all dead."

I didn't stop to ask questions. I knew in my heart that Bob was dead. That was enough for me. My horse was damned near up to full speed before I was properly in the saddle. As I slung my right leg over I felt a searing pain in my right butt and almost fell off. Broadwell, riding right behind me, called out, "I'm hit, Flo. I'm hit, again."

I looked back and saw him fall sideways off his horse. His left foot caught in a stirrup as he fell so his horse dragged him along a few yards until it came free. I had problems of my own. I caught another bullet in the fleshy part of my left arm, above the elbow. That hurt almost as much as the one in my ass. Broadwell's horse, no longer burdened by his weight, caught up with me. We raced out of town, side by side until the horses staggered to a halt in a shallow draw.

I slid down off my horse and checked my wounds. They were both flesh wounds; no bones broken, but they were bleeding fast and they hurt like hell. I tied my kerchief around the one in my arm and stuffed a spare shirt into my pants to cover the four-inch-long gash on my butt. I rested there, with the two horses close by, for a couple of hours or more. Then, with the afternoon losing its grip on the day, I mounted up – oh, that hurt so much – and rode south. I figured if I took it slow and easy I could make it to Peggy and Claude's place by morning. That was the longest night of my life and the worst ride I had ever experienced.

I knew I was losing a lot of blood. I also knew I had to keep going, or die out there alone and in the open. My horse seemed to understand my pain. She made each step as gentle as she could. Holding on to her neck with both arms, I let her take the lead. Without complaint, she carried me south through the dark hours, always followed by Broadwell's mount, until she came to the farm. I guess that's when I rolled sideways out of the saddle, although I don't remember doing so.

When Claude and Clay walked out of the house in the early morning light to get their long work day started they found me slumped against the side of the barn covered in blood. My two horses stood close by, still saddled.

I came to as the guys carried me into Peggy's kitchen. I heard Claude say, "It's Flo. You know, Bob Dalton's girl. Get some water boiling, Peggy. She's hurt real bad."

I don't remember it but Peggy told me later that I kept moaning, "They're dead. They're all dead."

CHAPTER 12

Claude was right. I was hurt bad, plus I had lost a lot of blood on the overnight ride. Peggy bathed and cleaned my wounds, bandaged them and put me to bed, and there I stayed for the best part of two weeks. They told me I almost died a couple of times from fever, but Peggy would not give up on me. I think she forced me to live.

One evening, I think it was the second day after I got out of bed, we sat around the kitchen table and I told Peggy and Claude, and young Clay, the story of the Coffeeville raid. No one said a word until I finished and then Peggy looked at Claude, gave a nod and said, "When you all left here, we figured you were up to no good. There was so much tension between all of you, especially between Bob and Grat, and that was not Bob's way."

I stayed on at the ranch for another couple of weeks, slowly getting my strength back while my wounds healed. I helped Peggy where I could and I cleaned out the barn one day while the guys were out on the range. I walked my horses for an hour most days, then left them in a corral with Peggy's horse for company. Clay made it clear with his eyes and his body that he would sure have liked to play around with me but I had to put him off.

"Clay," I said, "much as I like you, and much as I enjoyed our get together a few weeks ago, I'm too damn sore all over for anything you have in mind."

The day I left was tough. Peggy cried. I cried. Claude and Clay both looked uncomfortable, but they shook my hand and smiled when I kissed both of them on the cheek.

"Where you headed for, Flo?" asked Claude.

"Better you don't know, any of you," I replied. "Someday a United States Marshall's gonna come calling and asking questions about the Daltons, and about me, probably. Better you know as little as possible."

Getting into the saddle was an exercise in pain control. Damn, it hurt as Claude helped me hoist myself up in a stirrup and swing my leg over. I sat down on the leather saddle as gently as I could but still felt tears in my eyes. My arm was mostly healed by then, just a bit sore still. I figured I would be able to work that out with some six-gun practice and with whip exercises. My butt would just have to get used to being painful for a while longer. I wasn't planning to use it for any romping in the hay yet, as far as I knew. I reckoned Dick Broadwell's mount would never be recognized, so I left it with Claude and Peggy as an extra thanks for looking after me.

I gave Peggy a smile and a small wave. I knew that I could never come back – it wouldn't be fair to any of them. But I knew I was gonna miss Peggy's smiling face, her cooking and her lively chat. I sure would have liked to have that lady as my mother, or sister.

I had thought about going to the bunkhouse at the Mashed-O and resting for another week. Once I got my head cleared, I knew that would not be smart. If the lawmen were looking for me, they'd be sure to hit the Mashed-O. The one place I could think of where I'd be safe, and no danger to anyone else, was the one place I had refused to go with Bob.

"I'm not living with you in a damned cave!" I remembered saying it so well. Now, with two bullet wounds trying to heal and the law probably on my trail, the cave had to be the best place to hide. I rode in a semicircle to get there, turning back on my tracks a few times, taking to the rocks and leading my mare over the stones so no obvious signs would be left. When I got close to the cave my horse got scared. She whinnied and she bucked.

"Whoa, girl. It's okay," I tried to sooth her. "There's no one in there. Nothing to be afraid of."

As if to prove me wrong, a shadow passed across the mouth of the cave and a deep, guttural cough sounded followed by a loud chirruping. I'd heard that sound before. It spelled danger. The cougar appeared in the entrance, looking straight at us. My horse reared up, almost throwing me off. By the time I had her under control again the cougar had gone – but where?

There was no way I could go into the cave after that, and I certainly couldn't stay there, whether the big cat was still there or not. It could come back at any time. Anyway, my horse had no intention of staying. We turned away and made camp a few miles beyond in the shelter of some big boulders. As a precaution, I hobbled my horse. I could not afford to have her run away while I slept beside my small fire.

I still had some money left from one of our late summer raids so I decided the best place to hide for a few days would be a hotel. The nearest hotel, of course, was in Coffeeville. I thought about that for a morning while waiting for the sun to warm me. Coffeeville? Hmm. That just might be the one place where I could hide in the open. The only person who had taken a good look at me was the kid driving the wagon that parked in the lane behind Slosson's, and he would not have known I was part of the gang of robbers. No one else had even noticed me. The risk, it seemed, was worth it. I turned my horse to the north-east once more and rode slowly back to Coffeeville.

CHAPTER 13

Nothing much had changed in the weeks since the raid. Walnut Street was tidier. The hitching rail outside McCoy's Hardware was back in place where it should have been on that painful morning in October. I could see what looked like bullet holes in some of the buildings.

The folks were going about their daily business. A few buckboards rolled past me. Two men stood talking outside the Condon Bank. Three women walked arm in arm past the alley of death towards 9th Street. Kids played in the street. Across the other side a man was getting his whiskers trimmed at Smith's Barbershop. It looked like a normal day to me.

As I rode my horse up to the hotel a sheriff came out of Slosson's. He stopped and took a long look at me, perhaps surprised that I was dressed like a man but my long hair was hanging loose down my back, making it obvious that I was a woman. For a moment, I thought he had recognized me; then he smiled and touched the brim of his hat.

"'Morning, ma'am," he said. "A fine day to be out riding, ain't it?"

With that he walked in the opposite direction whistling to himself. He looked back once, that was all.

I had all but stopped breathing for a few minutes until the danger passed. With my heart beating like a drum, I stabled my horse and entered the hotel. I was lucky, they had a room overlooking the lane and it was available for as long as I wanted. I said I would be staying about a week. The chatty clerk asked me what I was doing in town. I stopped that conversation by asking about a bath. A couple of hours later I walked out the front door and into bright sunshine and went shopping. Soon after, wearing my new best dress and bonnet, with a parasol in one hand and a purse in the other, I was just another well-dressed lady out for a stroll on a lovely day. For the first time in weeks, I felt good. Maybe the thrill of taking a risk helped.

I didn't expect any trouble but, just to be safe, I had a loaded Derringer in my purse. It wasn't much of a weapon, unless used close up, even so, it was better than nothing. The sheriff passed me again near the First National Bank. He failed to recognize me as the rider he had seen earlier that morning. He just gave me another smile; a cheerful, "Howdy, ma'am." He added a nice compliment about my bonnet and went on his way.

Over the next few days I walked all over Coffeeville. I followed the route we had taken in on that day of disaster. I strolled along the alley where I had kept the horse. I looked through the windows of both banks. No robbers in town that day. Everything was back to a normal prairie town routine.

Almost a week after I arrived in the town I packed away my dresses and bonnet, and my parasol. Dressed in my usual outfit of shirt, long pants, chaps, boots and my Stetson I rode out to the cemetery. There were no markers for the fallen members of the Dalton gang. I searched until I found four fresh graves close together, without flowers and no headstones. Those, I knew, had to be the final resting places of Bob and Grat, Bill Powers and Dick Broadwell. With no way of knowing which grave held Bob's body, I just stood there in silence, looking from one to the other. Then, with a shake of my head, I said, "Idiots!" and went back to my horse. It was time for me to leave that sad chapter in my life where it belonged: far behind me.

THE SIXTH MAN

CHAPTER 14

Well, that's all in the past. As far as I know, there's just me left from the Dalton gang now. I heard that Bill Dalton, who was never really part of the gang, was killed by a Deputy U.S. Marshall outside his own home near Elk, Oklahoma. I knew that Emmett was still alive but he was living a normal life. He spent fifteen years in Lansing jail for his part in the Coffeeville job and that changed him. Soon after he got his freedom back he married and moved to California. I thought about going to see him there but I figured it was too far to go for old time's sake. Emmett was no longer an outlaw, but I am: still an outlaw, I mean.

I missed Bob for a long time. I missed those blue eyes and I missed the action, in and out of bed. Yes, even now, years after Coffeeville, I still miss that dangerous bastard, but I don't dwell on it. I grew up to be tough and I've learned to be tougher still – and I've got the bullet scars to prove it. I'm the kind of woman you just can't keep down, unless I want you on top of me for a while, of course. And then, well, you'd better be ready because I'll treat you to a ride that'll keep you saddle sore but smiling for many long days.

So many years have passed since the pointless tragedy at Coffeeville. Now, in early October 1912, I live quietly these days in a small, one-storey wooden house outside of Deadwood, South Dakota. I'm far enough from town for peace and quiet but close enough if I feel like some action – which I still enjoy occasionally. I've been holed up here for a couple of years now. I mind my own business and no one bothers me. I needed somewhere to lay low for a while after a couple of minor indiscretions – you know – a couple or more horses that somehow ended up in my care without the owners' permissions. I bought this place under a different name and use both, the house and the name, to hide from the law and to write my story – and my version of the Coffeyville fiasco as perpetrated by the Dalton gang. The story's just about finished now…

A commotion of horse's hooves, rare at any time this far out of town, disturbed my concentration. I put down my pen for a few minutes and looked out the window.

"Oh, shee-it," I breathed out.

Six mounted men galloped up to the house, each one holding a rifle at the ready. Their horses stamped their feet in the dust as they turned in a line to face my front door. I recognized one as a U.S. Marshall by his badge and knew this could be the final showdown.

"Come on out, Flo, or we'll come in and get you," the Marshall shouted.

"Just a minute while I get dressed," I yelled back to stall them.

I ran back to my table and scribbled these last few words in the hope that someone will be able to read them some day.

EPILOGUE

Howdy, folks. Deputy United States Marshall Heck Thomas here again. Now that the long chase is over, let me tell you about Flo Quick's last moments. They were exciting, frightening and bloody – typical of the way she lived.

A few minutes after I called out to her, Flo sauntered out onto her veranda as if she had all the time in the world. The two top buttons of her shirt were open – that's the first thing we saw. She leaned forward a little so we all had a good look at some mighty fine white flesh. She straightened up slowly and tipped her black Stetson up off her brow. I noticed she was taller than I had expected, and she sure was pretty. In her left hand she carried that damn bull-whip I'd heard so much about. There was a holstered six-gun slung low on her right thigh, but her hand was on her hip.

"Well, howdy, boys," she crooned at us. "What a surprise to see you all." Then, looking me straight in the eyes, she added, "Hello, Marshall. I'll bet your name's Heck Thomas. Ain't it?"

I nodded and answered, my voice almost quiet, "That's almost right, ma'am. Deputy U.S. Marshall Heck Thomas is my name, not Marshall. Now, if you'll just drop your gun and step down here…"

That's as far as I got. Flo smiled at me and shook her head. She took off her Stetson and fanned her face before replacing it with the brim now tilted over her eyes.

"Well," she said, "it's all the same to me, Mister Deputy U.S. Marshall Heck Thomas. Huh! Marshall? Deputy Marshall? It's all the same to this gal."

She walked, long-legged and sexy, the length of the veranda. All the time her eyes flickered over the men in my posse and back to me. She turned and sauntered back to her starting point. Her smile stretched across her face.

"Heck? Now where'd you get a name like that?" she crooned. "I'll just bet your momma looked down between her legs when you were being born and said to herself, oh, heck, this one's gonna be a lawman. Am I right, Mister Deputy U.S. Marshall Heck Thomas?"

A couple of my men sniggered but I soon cut them off without a glance.

"Shut up, all of you," I ordered. "This ain't no laughing matter."

That Flo was a cocky witch. She strutted the lengthy of her veranda again and back with a gorgeous smile on her face. I could see what she was doing. She was deliberately distracting my men so she could strike without warning. Just like a rattler. She stopped and looked me right in the eyes. Her smile was bright and dangerous.

"Hot, ain't it? Hot as Heck," Flo drawled. Her right hand strayed up towards her cleavage and undid a couple more buttons. I thought she was about to release both her goodies at once but somehow the shirt held them in – just.

"Now, what can I do for you fine looking gentlemen?" she purred.

Her right hand dropped slowly, closer to her hip and hovered just above the six-gun. The left hand moved the coils of her whip in a small circle.

"Drop the gun, Flo, just like I asked you," I called. "Slow and easy now, ma'am, and no one need get hurt. Take it out with thumb and forefinger and toss it over here."

Charlie Smithson, a good man to have on a posse but sometimes a mouthy jerk, shouted, "And keep that damned whip still, iffen you know what's good for you."

Flo didn't look at him or acknowledge him in any way. She leaned forward again, showing a lot more flesh as she reached for the six-gun: thumb and forefinger only, just like I told her. Trouble is we were all trying to concentrate on that gun and watch her chest at the same time and forgot about the whip. Before we knew it, the rattlesnake had struck. That whip shot out and wrapped itself around Charlie's neck with a crack like a rifle shot. Flo heaved with one hand and Charlie was dragged off his horse fast: dead before he hit the ground.

I came to my senses first and fired at where Flo had been, but she was rolling across the veranda in a ball. When she came up she had the six-gun in her right hand and it was already smoking. Two of my boys had gone down in quick succession and two more screamed in pain as Flo's next slugs tore into them. The horses were bucking all over the place, even mine, but I managed to get off one lucky shot from my Winchester and hit Flo right through one of the beautiful mounds of flesh she

THE SIXTH MAN

had used to tempt us. The bullet tore through the softness and slammed into her heart. The impact threw her backwards over the side rail of the veranda and down she went. Down and out. I looked around me. Three of my men were dead – one from a broken neck and two from hot lead. Two others were wounded, one in the leg and the other in the gut. I was the only one left on horse-back and, once I stopped shaking, I figured I was just plain lucky.

As soon as I had the boys fixed up in town by the local doc, I went back to Flo's house for a look around. I found this book manuscript on her table and read it through at one sitting, while drinking her coffee laced with some whiskey I found in a cupboard. It's a hell of a story and it sure answered a lot of questions for me, especially about the Daltons and the raid on the Coffeeville banks. Most of all though it is Flo's story and it does her proud. She had a great sense of humor and she makes no apologies about her life-style or the men she rode with. I tell you, that Flo Quick was one hellfire of a she-cat and sexy with it. What a woman. What a waste of a real woman.

We buried her at Boot Hill just outside of Deadwood a few days later – the same graveyard that already held the remains of Wild Bill Hickok and Calamity Jane. No one knew her real name or her age, or anything else about her, so we carved Florence Quick on the marker with the date of her death and left it at that. The whole damned community of near two hundred people came out to say goodbye as if we were burying some kind of a heroine, instead of a murderer and common thief. As the undertaker and gravediggers started shoveling dirt down on her plain wooden coffin, I couldn't help thinking that we had reached the end of an era. Flo Quick, an outlaw for well over half of her forty-something years, was dead. She had lived life in her own style and, as the preacher said when she was being lowered into her grave, "She was part of the history of the American west and she died in a blaze of glory."

I agree about the history, but I'm not so sure about the glory part. However, Flo Quick sure did go out in a blaze of fire: gun fire, the hot and deadly kind – just like she was.

The end

ABOUT THE AUTHOR

Anthony Dalton is a Fellow of the Royal Geographical Society and a Fellow of the Royal Canadian Geographical Society. He is the award-winning author of 14 non-fiction books, most about the sea or about exploration, and two earlier novels. A past President of the Canadian Authors Association, and an accomplished public speaker, he is an historian and former expedition leader. He lives in the Southern Gulf Islands of British Columbia, Canada, with his wife Penny and a yellow Labrador named Rufus.

More historical fiction from Anthony Dalton

THE MATHEMATICIAN'S JOURNEY
Part 1 of *The Hudson Bay Trilogy*.

The icy world of Captain Henry Hudson, doomed 17th century Arctic explorer, comes alive in this compelling novel.

Narrated by Thomas Woodhouse, a young mathematician and sailor, we meet his well-to-do English family and a lady friend. He takes us with him to Oxford University and he shares his passion for Arctic exploration.

Signed on board Hudson's expedition ship Discovery for a voyage in search of the North-West Passage, Thomas works with a disparate crew and experiences the erratic mind of their commanding officer.

Thomas's adventurous story ranges across southern England, the North Atlantic Ocean, the sub-Arctic, the wilderness forests of eastern Canada and part of old France.

PRAISE FOR

THE MATHEMATICIAN'S JOURNEY

"Anthony Dalton is himself no stranger to the Arctic or sailing. He brings that knowledge to bear in his meticulously researched historical novel to take the reader on a voyage of discovery from the peaceful cloisters of Oxford of King James I's England to the Atlantic wastes and the frigid waters of what will come to be known as Hudson Bay thence to a native village and finally, after many years, back to upper class London. Peopled with three-dimensional characters set against vividly described backgrounds the plot will keep you turning the pages and at book's end hoping the hero's adventures will continue in another work."

Patrick Taylor
New York Times best-selling author
of the *Irish Country Doctor* series

THE SIXTH MAN

More books by Anthony Dalton

Fiction
The Mathematician's Journey
Relentless Pursuit

Non-fiction
Henry Hudson
Sir John Franklin
Fire Canoes
The Fur-Trade Fleet
Polar Bears
Adventures with Camera and Pen
A Long, Dangerous Coastline
Graveyard of the Pacific
Arctic Naturalist, the life of J. Dewey Soper
River Rough, River Smooth
Alone Against the Arctic
Baychimo, Arctic Ghost Ship
J/Boats Sailing to Success
Wayward Sailor, in Search of the Real Tristan Jones

All books are available from Amazon.com; Barnes & Noble, and the publishers' websites. Also see
www.anthonydalton.net
www.themathematiciansjourney.com